DOUBLE TROUBLE IN BUGLAND

William Kotzwinkle

Double Trouble
in Bugland

PROFUSELY ILLUSTRATED BY
Joe Servello

❈

DAVID R. GODINE, PUBLISHER
Boston

First published in 2016 by
DAVID R. GODINE, PUBLISHER, INC.
Post Office Box 450
Jaffrey, New Hampshire 03452

For permissions contact
DAVID R. GODINE, PUBLISHER,
Fifteen Court Square, Suite 320,
Boston, Massachusetts 02108.

LIBRARY OF CONGRESS CATALOGING IN PUBLICATION DATA
Names: Kotzwinkle, William, author. | Servello, Joe, illustrator.
Title: Double Trouble in Bugland / by William Kotzwinkle ; illustrated by Joe Servello.
Description: Jaffrey, New Hampshire : David R. Godine, 2016. | Sequel to: Trouble in
Bugland. | Summary: Inspector Mantis and Dr. Hopper exercise their powers of deduction as
they face more deadly foes than ever in these four tales of mystery and murder in Bugland.
Identifiers: LCCN 2015050687| ISBN 9781567925647 (alk. paper) | ISBN 1567925642
Subjects: | CYAC: Mystery and Detective Stories. | Insects–Fiction.
Classification: LCC PZ7.K855 Dou 2016 | DDC [Fic]–dc22
LC record available at https://lccn.loc.gov/2015050687
ISBN 978-1-56792-564-7

First Edition
PRINTED IN CHINA

Contents

THE CASE OF THE LONELY VAMPIRE

THE LITTLE FLAT on Flea Street was undergoing spring-cleaning. Mrs. Inchworm had taken all of Inspector Mantis's chemical apparatus into the hallway, much to his displeasure. But the landlady was insistent. "This stuff is filthy, Inspector Mantis, you never dust it."

"It is not necessary to dust it, Mrs. Inchworm," groaned the detective, as he watched her shoving out his tubes and beakers and burners.

"A body can't clean properly with all this mess around," she said, and tossed his chemistry notebooks into a pile in the hallway.

"Doctor, stop her," cried Mantis.

"I've got all I can do defending my own corner, Mantis," said Hopper, whose popcorn popper was now on the way into the hall, along with his fudge pans. "Please, Mrs. Inchworm, that popcorn popper is a delicate instrument."

"It's stuck up with butter and salt. The pair of you are impossible. Everything you have is a mess, and these rooms are a complete jumble."

"I shall never be able to find anything now," moaned Mantis. "I am ruined."

"Don't step where I've mopped or I'll give you what-for."

"Oh bother," said Mrs. Inchworm, "you'll manage just fine. And everything will be sparkling clean." She turned abruptly in the hall, facing the stairs. "Who are you?"

A timid looking bug stood at the top of the stairs, hat in hand. "Titus Toe-biter. I'm here to see Inspector Mantis."

"Well, he can't see you now. He's spring-cleaning."

"I'm doing nothing of the kind," said Mantis, from the doorway. "Please, Mr. Toe-biter, come in."

Toe-biter edged his way nervously past Mrs. Inchworm. "Begging your pardon, ma'am—"

"Don't step where I've mopped or I'll give you what-for."

"No, certainly not, I wouldn't dream of it," said the intimidated bug. He entered the room and Mantis gestured him toward the window seat, for all of the furniture was piled in one corner and was inaccessible.

"You must forgive the upset, Toe-biter. Mrs. Inchworm is relentless in springtime."

"Oh sir, I understand," said Toe-biter softly, with a nervous, sideways glance toward Mrs. Inchworm. "My landlady is a fierce housekeeper," he continued in an ever lower voice. "She turns the place upside down, and I can't find so much as a postage stamp afterwards."

"More than a postage stamp is at stake here," said Mantis, loudly enough for Mrs. Inchworm to hear. "Experiments, fragile and extremely complicated in their makeup, have been completely destroyed."

"It smells like a lot of rotten eggs," said Mrs. Inchworm. "How valuable could that be?"

"Of incalculable value, Mrs. Inchworm." Mantis returned his gaze to his visitor. "Toe-biter, this is Doctor Hopper, who assists me in my cases. You may speak freely in front of him."

"Thank you, Inspector Mantis. I'm pleased to have two such distinguished gentlemen as yourself helping me."

"If we can, Toe-biter. But first we must know what your problem is."

"Murder, Inspector Mantis. Or the next thing to it."

Mantis's eyes lit up, and his chemical experiments were forgotten that instant. Mrs. Inchworm could have thrown them into the street or hammered them to bits, for Mantis cared for them no longer. All of his keen powers of concentration were riveted on Titus Toe-biter. "Tell us more, and leave nothing out."

"Well, sir," said Toe-biter, "I've come into the city from my little village."

"Which is East Gum Leaf."

The eyes of the visitor widened. "But how—"

"The gum tree has the annoying habit of exuding its gum onto the clothing of passersby." Mantis reached out, and extracted a bit of gum from Toe-biter's sleeve. "But I'm sorry. You were saying?"

"Well, yes, as you say—I'm from East Gum Leaf. A sweeter little village you couldn't find anywhere. Until recently."

"Lift your feet," said Mrs. Inchworm, coming by with her broom.

"Mrs. Inchworm, I am conducting an interview."

"That's it, gentlemen, everyone's feet in the air, very good. Now see how much nicer the floor looks."

"It looks exactly as it looked before," said Mantis.

"Then you must be blind." Mrs. Inchworm pointed to the window seat. "Now stand up, please, I must shake out those cushions."

"Really, Mrs. Inchworm, this is intolerable."

"It happens once a year. You'll survive it." And she hammered the cushions with the flat of her hand. "Look at the dust flying out of them."

Mantis lowered his head to his chest, and closed his eyes. He appeared to be counting under his breath.

Mrs. Inchworm fluffed out the cushions and set them back on the window seat. "There now, that's better."

"I can see no discernible difference," said Mantis.

"And you the great detective," said Mrs. Inchworm. "It's a wonder you can solve anything." She laid a hand on Titus Toe-biter's sleeve. "There now, Mr. Toe-biter, you go ahead. You were saying how nice your village is."

Titus Toe-biter smiled weakly. "Yes, it is. Or was. Until the Vampire came."

"Dear me," said Mrs. Inchworm.

"Vampire?" asked Mantis. "But there is no such thing."

"I'm telling you, the Vampire sucked the life out of my dear old friend, Angus Earwig. And tossed him aside like a dried-up gum leaf."

"Have the police investigated this matter?"

"Oh, yes. Without finding anything, of course. Because they wouldn't believe me when I said Angus was murdered by the Vampire."

"And who do they suspect?" asked Doctor Hopper.

"They said it could have been an assassin bug, settling a political score. There's your motive, they said, no need to drag in the supernatural. But Angus Earwig was about as political as that popcorn popper. The Vampire killed him!"

"And why do you say that, Mr. Toe-Biter?"

"Because I saw it!" And saying this, Toe-biter drew back slightly from the window, as if fearing the Vampire was hovering outside it.

"What exactly did you see?" asked Doctor Hopper.

"Other side of the room, gentlemen," said Mrs. Inchworm, "I must wash that window."

"Mrs. Inchworm, I hereby give you my notice," said Mantis. "I shall seek lodgings elsewhere."

"I've heard that before." Mrs. Inchworm dragged over her bucket and sponge. "Now, if you would please—there's plenty of room for a chat over there." She gestured vaguely.

"Where, pray? In the fireplace? Should I conduct my interview on hot coals?"

"I can't believe the filth of this window," said Mrs. Inchworm. "Some kind of scummy cloud from your test tubes, I suppose." She sniffed it, and looked toward Doctor Hopper. "No, it smells like fudge."

"There was a small explosion in the fudge pan, yes."

"Did it occur to you to clean it up?"

"I can't believe the filth of this window"

"A complete scouring of the area was performed," said Hopper. "There's fudge on the curtains too. Well, these will have to come down and be washed." Mrs. Inchworm brought over her step-stool, and went up it, as Mantis, Hopper, and Toe-biter removed themselves to the other side of the room, where they found seats on stacks of magazines.

"Pray continue, Toe-biter," said Mantis. "You were about to tell us what you saw."

"Well," said Toe-biter, "it was nighttime. That's when we Toe-biters like to go out for a little nip."

"Quite," said Mantis.

"Now toe-biting's not really dangerous but it does require a certain amount of stealth."

"Yes, yes," said Mantis, somewhat impatiently, for the drink-and-dining habits of every creature in Bugland was known to him in detail.

"Well, as I say, I'd had a nip or two and was on my way home. And I suddenly got an impulse to visit my old friend, Angus Earwig. I went up to his room—he just had the one room over a horsefly stable, there was nothing fancy about Angus—and I went up to his door and knocked. There wasn't any answer so I opened the door and went in. And there was Angus stretched out on the floor and the Vampire going out the window."

"My, my," said Mrs. Inchworm, having come to listen beside them.

"Return to your cleaning, Mrs. Inchworm," said Mantis, cuttingly. "I should think nothing on earth could deter you from it."

"Oh, I need a little break. And poor Mr. Toe-biter, finding his friend stretched out like that."

"Yes," continued Toe-biter, "it was a terrible shock. But far more terrible was the sight of that cloaked figure hurrying toward the open window. It was all in black velvet, and the collar of its cloak was high, to hide its face. Then it staggered, drunkenly I imagine, from poor old Angus's blood. It twisted toward me, and I saw a chain of gold at its collar, holding shut the cloak. And its face—oh that face..."

"Now, now, Mr. Toe-biter, don't upset yourself," said Mrs. Inchworm. "Have a piece of Doctor Hopper's fudge."

"Mrs. Inchworm," said Hopper, "where did you find that fudge? I thought there was none left."

"There was a great gob of it behind the gramaphone."

"Remarkable," said Hopper.

"And on the wall."

"The force of the explosion was greater than I thought."

"*Might* we," snarled Mantis, "drop fudge as our focus, and return to the facts of this case?"

"Show some feeling, Inspector Mantis," said Mrs. Inchworm. "He needs that bite of fudge to buck him up."

"I'm all right now," said Titus Toe-biter. "It was just the memory of the Vampire's face—"

"And what was it about the face, Toe-biter?" asked Mantis.

"The leering, awful grin it had, Inspector Mantis. It was enjoying the terrible thing it'd just done to poor old Angus."

"And something else?" prodded Mantis.

"And this, Inspector Mantis—that face seemed as old as the hills, as old as time. As if it had lived forever on the blood of the innocent."

"Heavens," said Mrs. Inchworm, "that sends a chill right through me."

"It may feed on the blood of the innocent, Mrs. Inchworm," said Mantis, "but it does not live forever."

"Well, how do you *know*?"

"Because I am a scientist." Mantis stuffed his hands into the pockets of his dressing gown. "And for science there can be no such thing as a Vampire who lives forever."

"Well, poor Mr. Toe-biter here is shaking like a leaf just thinking of what he saw."

Mantis turned to Toe-biter. "I am taking on your case, Toe-biter. You may stop shaking."

"Thank you, sir. I wish I could."

"Give him more fudge, Mrs. Inchworm," said Mantis.

Doctor Hopper sat upright. "Mantis, I've never known you to endorse fudge before."

"I have learned from you, Doctor, its soothing properties."

"A sovereign remedy," nodded Hopper, "even when exploded into irregular shapes."

"Shape doesn't matter to me," said Titus Toe-biter, gnawing on the fudge. "I like it fine. And I believe it has calmed me down."

"Then let us be off to East Gum Leaf," said Mantis. "Mrs. Inchworm, you may finish your dusting."

"You know, gentlemen," said Mrs. Inchworm, "I'd have much less dusting to do if you two would do a little of it yourself after you finish your fudge experiments."

"I do not experiment with fudge," said Mantis. "And dusting is out of the question."

"Mantis, really," said Hopper, "we should pitch in if that's what Mrs. Inchworm wants."

"Very well," said Mantis, with an air of one who gives a great deal. "I shall dust the dart board. Every day. Religiously."

Doctor Hopper smiled apologetically at Mrs. Inchworm. "He's a proud creature, Mrs. Inchworm. He must start humbly."

"I'm pleased if he starts anywhere at all."

"And you, Doctor," said Mantis. "With what shall you start?"

"Why, the fudge pans, of course. They must be kept sparkling clean. I admit to having been lax in that matter." He turned to his landlady. "Mrs. Inchworm, you'll have no cause to complain about dust in the fudge pans."

"You're hopeless, the pair of you," said Mrs. Inchworm. "Go and catch your Vampire."

"That, dear lady," said Mantis, "I can promise you."

〔 ☀ 〕

THE TRAIN PULLED into East Gum Leaf, and Mantis, Hopper, and Titus Toe-biter stepped down onto the platform. "Ah, my sweet little village," said Toe-biter. "How good it is to get back." And then a shadow crossed his face, as harsh memory surfaced. "Sucking the blood of the innocent..." He stared off into space.

"Snap out of it, Toe-biter," said Mantis. "After all, you yourself bite the toes of sleepers."

"But I just take a little nip! No one misses it. The worst they have is an itchy toe." But even in this protest, the fear did not leave Toe-biter's face. "I do not suck the life out of people. I do not leave them behind like empty husks." And again a shudder ran through him as he thought of Angus Earwig stretched out on the floor. "You haven't seen what I've seen, Inspector Mantis."

"I've seen a great deal."

"Well, I suppose you have. And that's why I called on you to help me. To help this whole village."

"Well, Toe-biter, I suggest we visit the room where Angus Earwig perished."

"Yes, all right. It's not far. We can walk."

The three bugs strode through the village. No more peaceful spot could be imagined, with its little shops and its narrow winding lanes. "I say, Mantis," said Hopper, "here's a candy shop. It might be wise to purchase a few provisions."

"As you wish, Doctor," said Mantis.

"Decent of you, old man. It won't take a moment." Hopper entered the shop and stepped into the familiar smell of chocolate. But heavier than the scent of chocolate in the air was a feeling of terror. It seemed to emanate from the very walls of the shop, and most certainly from the eyes of the shop's proprietor. She was a honeypot ant, and she was trembling as she peeked out from behind a back curtain of the shop.

"Can I help you?" she asked, in a voice that quivered with fear.

"My dear lady," said Hopper, "you're in terrible distress."

"Ah, my sweet little village," said Toe-biter. *"How good it is to get back."*

"So I am, sir," said the honeypot. "So is everyone in the village. We're afraid to step outside our doors. Not that it matters." Here the honeypot shuddered. "For the Vampire can kill you indoors as well as out."

"He shall kill no one, my good woman, while I am here."

"Oh, sir, are you from the police?"

"I am assisting Inspector Mantis, the consulting detective who is at work on this case."

"Is he the tall fellow standing outside?"

"That is Mantis, yes."

"He looks like a deep one."

"He is deep, Madame. And absolutely fearless, I assure you."

"Oh, he'd better be. The Vampire can scare the life out of someone just by looking at them."

"Inspector Mantis will deal with this so-called Vampire, Madame. And I myself shall not be idle in the matter. To that end, may I have an assorted bag of candy? I use it as an aid to concentration."

"Certainly, sir." The honeypot inserted a little scoop into each of the candy bins and filled a paper bag to the top. "It's hand-made. Me and my sisters, we put a little bit of ourselves in every piece of it. We're naturally sweet, you know."

"Indeed, you are," said Hopper. If one merely stroked a honeypot's antenna, a sweet excrescence would appear on her lips. One drop of that divinely pure substance was enough for an entire batch of candy.

"Here you are, sir. And when you finish that, I've got plenty more."

"I shall certainly return when I run out, thank you. By the way, did you know Angus Earwig?"

"I did, sir. He was murdered in his bed. By the Vampire."

"And did anyone see in which direction the Vampire went after he left Earwig's bedroom?"

"I'm sure I don't know, sir, and I don't want to know." The honeypot had begun trembling again.

"No, of course not. Forgive me for asking. Well, good-day to you."

Hopper went out beneath the tinkling bell and rejoined Mantis in the street. "Sorry, old man, I was fishing for information."

"And?"

"The candy is hand-made."

"*That* is most helpful."

"Best I could do, Mantis. She knows nothing."

"She's frightened," said Toe-biter. "We're all frightened. We're afraid to go to bed at night." He glanced back over his shoulder, for the day was drawing to a close, and the hour of the Vampire was drawing near.

"I see you are uneasy," said Mantis.

"I'll be sitting up until morning in a chair. It has me worn out, I'll tell you. And that could be dangerous. I mean, if I go crawling in around a bunch of toes when I'm dead tired, I could get careless. I could fall asleep right there on the end of a big toe."

"Heaven forbid," said Doctor Hopper, concern in his voice. As a medical practitioner he'd seen his share of vocational accidents, caused by bugs sleeping on the job.

"If I'm all tuckered out, I could get squashed all right, by some itchy sleeper. And what should have been an easy night's work would be my last night's work."

"Then you must not work until you're rested," said Hopper.

"I've got to eat, Doctor."

"Then have some candy."

"Thank you, I shall. All right, here's Angus Earwig's rooming house."

They entered the humble dwelling and climbed the stairs to the scene of the crime—the dead bug's room.

Mantis began a thorough search of the room. From floor to ceiling, nothing went unexamined.

"I hate it in here," said Toe-biter to Hopper. "The feel of that Vampire is still in the air."

"Have another piece of candy, Toe-biter. Steady your nerves."

"My nerves are ruined, Doctor Hopper. I've seen a fiend."

Mantis had his magnifying glass out and was going carefully over the window sill. He turned to Hopper. "Nothing. No trace of fibers, no imprints, no secretion. What have I missed?" He continued his search with an air of frustration.

"You'll not find anything," said Toe-biter. "Fiends don't leave any trace."

Mantis glared at him and continued his examination. "There are no fiends, Toe-biter. We must not allow ourselves to succumb to superstition."

"Poor old Earwig," said Toe-biter, staring at the bed where his friend had been slain. "We'd be playing a nice little game of checkers about now. With a pot of tea and a plate of cookies."

"Yes," said Doctor Hopper, "this is the hour when a cookie means a lot to a chap. Failing that, we have candy." He popped a chocolate nougat into his mouth. "I say, Mantis, this is excellent. Won't you have some?"

But Inspector Mantis seemed not to hear. He was on his knees, staring at a patch of carpet. "What have we here?" he asked in a low voice. He took a tweezers from his pocket, and with the aid of his magnifying glass, bent still closer to the carpet. "Is it...yes!" He struck with the tweezers, and held it up to the light of Earwig's table lamp.

"What have you got, Mantis?" asked Hopper.

"It could be nothing." Mantis took a small collecting box from his coat and opened it. A tiny, glittering object fell from the end of the tweezers into the box. He snapped it shut and slipped it into his pocket. "Or it could be everything, Doctor." He turned to Toe-biter. "Was Angus Earwig accustomed to having visitors, other than yourself?"

"No. So far as I know, I was the only friend he had."

"There is no housekeeper?"

"No."

"And the local police, the ones who were in the room after the murder—they are all flatfoot flies?"

"Yes, that's it. Nothing unusual about those lads."

"Very well, gentlemen, since it is tea time I suggest you go and have some. I must return to the city. I shall meet you back here at midnight."

A T THE TEA SHOP, Toe-biter remained silent, staring into his tea-cup. His tea grew cold and his tea cake went uneaten. "I say, Toe-biter," said Doctor Hopper, "if you're not going to eat that cake—"

"I haven't got the appetite, Doctor. Soon it will be dark, and then the trouble starts."

"Toe-biter, Mantis and I are with you on this." Hopper scooped up the cake. "No harm will come to you."

"You can't stop it, Doctor. Much as you might try."

"A jolly good knock on the head with this cane—" Hopper slapped it into his hand. "—will go a long way toward discouraging anyone who tries to harm you."

"The Vampire laughs at that sort of thing. He waits until you sleep. We all have to sleep sooner or later. And then he comes."

Hopper gazed out the window of the tea shop at the last faint streaks of light in the sky. He was unable to stop a feeling of apprehension from creeping over him. There was only one remedy he knew for it. "Waitress, could we please have a bit more cake at this table?"

M ANTIS WALKED along a darkened street, past little houses huddled together in a row. He stopped at a familiar rickety gate and entered a yard overgrown with weeds. He walked up a little pathway to the house, in which a single light burned. At the sound of his footstep on the stairs, a dogfly begin barking inside.

He rapped on the door, and waited. The dogfly yapped noisily, as muffled footsteps approached from within. "*Quiet, boy, be a good doggiefly.*" The door opened, but only slightly, a chain still across it. "Yes, who is it?"

"Inspector Mantis."

"Waitress, could we please have a bit more cake at this table?"

The chain clattered down and the door swung open. "Mantis! Upon my word!"

Professor Channing Booklouse stood within, a pair of old slippers on his feet, and wire-rimmed spectacles on the end of his nose. "Come in, come in. How good of you to call. How long has it been since we last saw each other? I think during that dreadful affair of the Admiralty secrets."

"It has been too long, Professor, forgive me."

"Ah well, you are busy, I know. As I am myself." Professor Booklouse led Mantis down a hallway lined with bookshelves, and the dogfly padded after them, sniffing at Mantis's heels.

"I was in the library, as you might have guessed," said Booklouse, and invited Mantis to step through to that room. Books went from floor to ceiling on all four walls, and a small stepladder was placed against one of the walls. "I was just eating my way through a little book of musical history—*The Life of Constantine Cicada*, the great tenor. A tasty volume, I must say. Constantine was a man of...irregular habits, if I may put it so. I feel quite giddy after ingesting it. He was brilliant, of course, but extremely eccentric. He wore a flowing wig and carried on with opera singers. But that isn't why you've come. Have a seat, please. Just throw those pamphlets on the floor, I'll be eating them later. Now what can I do for you?"

"I need information, Professor."

"And you shall have it, if it's within my power to provide it. Subject?"

"This." Mantis opened the collecting box and held it up to Booklouse. Booklouse adjusted his glasses and gazed at the small glittering object inside the box.

"Yes, I see. A good specimen, perfectly intact. We'll need magnification."

Mantis brought out his pocket glass, but Booklouse waved it off. "I've got a much stronger one than that." He led Mantis to his desk, where a huge magnifying glass was supported by a mechanical arm. "Put your specimen under it."

Mantis did so, and Booklouse lowered the arm directly over it. Then he peered through. "Very unusual. Have a look for yourself."

Mantis bent over the glass. Enormously magnified now, the object could be seen to be tapered at one end. The other end was divided into a row of jagged points. It was of a deep blue color.

"The color may not caused by pigment," said Booklouse. "It could be structural. We'll test for it later. It is the scale from a wing, of course."

"But whose wing?"

"Oh, a moth's, I'm pretty sure of that. But not one of ours. No, certainly not from a native of Bugland." He bent over the glass again. "This is from a most exotic creature. Foreign, possibly ancient?"

"Very much of the present, I'm afraid."

"All right, then, let me see—" Booklouse turned, adjusted his glasses once again, then strolled toward his bookshelves. Running the tip of his finger over the titles, he walked along a row of volumes. "So…so…so…yes…and…here…we…are."

He selected a volume and carried it over to his desk. "Now, let's see…be so good as to tilt the magnifying glass…yes, right there."

The iridescent blue scale was now visible to him, and he looked from it to the pages of his book as he made comparisons. On each page were large paintings of the scales of every moth and butterfly known to exist in Bugland and beyond. "Ah, what a dazzling display of beauty, Mantis. You and I are very plain bugs, I'm afraid."

"Quite."

"But we have our uses," chuckled Booklouse to himself. He had a quick eye, could quickly discern the differences in the various scales. "Here's one similar to your sample, but you see, along the edges…not quite it." And he turned the page to another display of shining wing scales. "Nothing here…no, not a thing…"

Mantis was disturbed at how rapidly Booklouse was going through the pages. "Booklouse, are you sure you're not missing anything?"

"Very unusual. Have a look for yourself."

"Absolutely, my dear fellow. There's not a scrap of similarity in any of these. Mustn't waste our time, you know. Now here's one that's more like it…but no, in at the center there, you see?"

"The shade of blue is not the same."

"Not the same at all. But we shan't let that discourage us. On we go, Mantis, down the next row. I do so like a good search. What is my library for, if not this?"

"You are a true scholar, Booklouse."

"Oh, I only nibble away at knowledge, Mantis, a little here, a little there. Now just a moment…I believe we might…yes…very good… you can see, of course…"

"You're in my way, Booklouse."

"So sorry. There, take a good look at *that*."

Mantis peered over the open page of the book, then over the sample beneath the magnifying glass. "It's the same."

"It's the same, at least superficially. However, we must be absolutely sure we're looking at structural color and not pigment." Booklouse brought out a dropper of clear liquid. "Alcohol. We must apply it to your sample."

Booklouse squeezed the bulb of the dropper and a single drop of alcohol fell on the shining blue scale. The hue changed markedly, then disappeared altogether. "Now, if it's a pigmented scale we have certainly ruined it and we'll never see color in it again. But if it's structural, if its color is caused by refraction of light playing in its grooves, alcohol can do it no permanent damage. We must wait a moment for it to dry. Can I give you a page of something to nibble on while we're waiting?"

"No, thank you."

"I've got a delicious volume of witty remarks made by theatrical personalities. The glue on the binding is quite the best I've ever tasted."

"I'm not hungry at the moment."

"And glue is not to everyone's liking, I know. Nor paper. But I have eaten some choice bits of antique parchment that would, I think, cause anyone's palate to water. Beautifully aged and having absorbed the damps and dews of countless sunrises and sunsets, wherein were contained the fragrances of flower and field, of pipe needles and apple blossoms, and a thousand other scents. Forgive me, I wax too fervently."

"Not at all."

"Old paper, Mantis, possesses a flakiness you cannot get from the new stuff. It melts on the tongue. It is pastry." Booklouse returned his gaze to the scale he'd soaked in alcohol. "There—the alcohol has evaporated. And you see—the color has completely returned. Proof of the structural nature of its origin. It creates color, as it were, by light refracting in these grooves, as if through a prism. That being so, we can be certain we have a definite match to the wing scale shown in this book."

Booklouse turned the page and read a description of the insect from whose wing the blue scale had fallen. "How disturbing."

"Indeed," said Mantis, reading over his shoulder.

"I should be careful if I were you." Booklouse put the scale back into its little container and handed it to Mantis. "The creature from whom this has come is one of the deadliest on earth."

"So it would seem."

"You are in pursuit of him?"

"I am." Mantis was hastily copying down essential details concerning the creature described in the book.

"Fortify yourself with a mouthful of old vellum. There's nothing like it for putting bounce in a fellow's step."

"Thank you, Booklouse, but I must go at once. Doctor Hopper is standing watch in dangerous circumstances."

"Give him my best, Mantis. And call on me again when I can be of assistance."

"I shall, Professor. And now goodnight. Don't get up, I know my way out."

Mantis departed, and Booklouse returned to his desk, where he stared at the page on which the iridescent blue scale was depicted. He shook his head and said softly to himself, "That such beauty should belong to one so deadly…ah well, that is part of life's mystery." He reached down and scratched behind the antennas of his faithful dogfly, who curled down at his feet and was presently asleep. Professor Booklouse ate a small pamphlet on arithmetic progression and was soon asleep himself, in his chair, hands folded across his little round belly.

INSPECTOR MANTIS'S next stop was in a fashionable side street of the city. There, shops of the better kind displayed their merchandise in window displays that were both tasteful and colorful. Mantis walked with a quick, sure step until he came to a shop whose sign identified it as Painted Lady Perfumes.

He entered, and a set of bells tinkled gently over the door frame. Behind the counter was a butterfly, with large blue-black spots on her wings. Mantis approached her directly. "You, I take it, are the painted lady?"

"Yes, monsieur, I am." The painted lady spoke with a marked French accent, and smiled flirtatiously at her tall, serious-looking customer. "How may I help you?"

"I'm looking for a scent."

"And I have them, whatever you wish." The painted lady turned, and pointed to the shelves behind her, which were filled with glittering bottles of every hue. "I have these, and many more." She stepped toward Mantis, fanning her wings. "Is it for your wife?"

"No," said Mantis, with some embarrassment. He rarely shopped, except for chemicals to be used in his experiments.

"Well, then, is it for your sweetheart? She'd probably like this. Smell it." The painted lady extended her wrist. "I'm wearing it myself."

Mantis, still more embarrassed, bent toward the lovely creature. A confirmed bachelor, and an irritable one, he was not in the habit of sniffing ladies' wrists. The scent caught him unaware. It was delicate, yet spicy; and the wrist on which it was offered was both slender and charming. Very charming, in fact, he said to himself, and took a

"You, I take it, are the painted lady?"

second sniff. He might even have taken a third sniff, so enjoyable was the experience, except he remembered why he was here. A murder had been committed. Another one could happen at any moment. He withdrew with a sudden jerk of his long neck.

"What's wrong, monsieur?" asked the painted lady, fanning her wings again, so that their tawny edges nearly touched him on the forehead. "Did something upset you?"

"No. I...remembered an appointment I must keep."

"With *her*, monsieur?" The painted lady smiled knowingly. "Well, then, we mustn't keep her waiting."

"No, we mustn't."

"So—do you like the scent I'm wearing?"

"Yes, it's very nice. But it's not the one I want. I'm looking for one that is more exotic."

"I have them all, monsieur. From every land. I have the scent that each bug uses to call to their beloved. Which one do you want?"

Mantis brought out the scrap of paper from his pocket, on which he'd copied a description of the creature from whom the blue wing scale had fallen. He placed it before the painted lady. "I wish to obtain the scent this bug secretes."

The painted lady put on an ornate pair of reading glasses, and read the scrap of paper. Now it was her turn to draw back sharply. She looked at Mantis. "You wish to attract this creature? But why?"

"I have no time to explain. Do you have the scent?"

"As I said, I have them all. It is my trade. Excuse me for one moment." The painted lady went through a beaded curtain, into a back room. Through the curtain Mantis could see her opening a cabinet. Dust flew from it as she did so. "I never have call for these—" she said, fanning the dust away with her wings. "They are the Perfumes of the Damned."

She looked through a shelf of bottles, finally selected one, and brought it out to Mantis. She placed it on the counter before him.

"There you are, monsieur." The bottle was small, of cut glass, many-sided. "I must ask you not to open it in here."

"I understand."

"There are certain customers I have no wish to attract."

"And yet you stock it."

"Just for you." The painted lady was no longer smiling. "I will not reorder it. To touch it makes me nervous."

"How much?"

"It may nearly have cost someone their life to gather it." The painted lady turned the bottle around, showing the price. "As you see, it is high."

Mantis withdrew his wallet. "I'll take it."

"I have something else that may interest you," said the painted lady. She went to the wall behind her and opened a safe. From it she brought out a rectangular jewel case which she laid on the counter. "It is from the same creature."

"Yes," said Mantis, "I must have this too."

"Be careful how you handle it," warned the painted lady, as he turned the jewel case over in his hand.

"I shall." Mantis counted out a large number of bills, including the rent money for this month, but there was no choice.

"I have the feeling you are not buying these items for love, monsieur."

"No, not love."

"For what, then?"

"Justice," said Mantis, and slipped the bottle and the jewel case into his pocket.

❦☀❦

IN EAST GUM LEAF, Doctor Hopper and Titus Toe-biter had gone back to Angus Earwig's room, where they now sat by the fire, making some popcorn. Hopper had insisted on this, saying that it would steady their nerves. "Nothing like gentle popping to produce peace-of-mind." Hopper shook the popping pan, swirling the kernels around.

"I've got no peace-of-mind," said Toe-biter. "I'm a nervous wreck. Look at the way my hand is shaking."

"Then you're the one who should be holding the popping pan." Hopper handed it to him and Toe-biter's hand shook so violently that the popcorn did pop more quickly and more evenly. When the popping was finished the popcorn was transferred to a large bowl.

"There," said Hopper, "and now we add a little butter and salt." Hopper poured and sprinkled, then gave the bowl a good stirring. "A bowl of hot, freshly buttered popcorn can get a bug through most anything."

"You've got a cheerful nature, Doctor. But I'm the gloomy sort."

"Nonsense. You've just had a bad fright." Hopper bit into a warm handful of popcorn and then shook the bowl under Toe-biter's nose. "Come on, Toe-biter, don't hold back."

With a sigh, Toe-biter took a few pieces, and then a few more, and finally began munching as steadily as Hopper. "I appreciate your being here, Doctor. I couldn't have faced it alone."

"Happy to be of service, Toe-biter. And of course, your case is a most interesting one."

Toe-biter stared at a few bits of popcorn in his lap. "It was the smile on that Vampire, Doctor. A smile that knew everything."

"Probably an effect of the light. And your horrified state, of course." Hopper licked a nice bit of butter from his finger.

"That look of his went right through me, Doctor. And he seemed to be saying, *you're next.*"

"Toe-biter, if he comes in here we'll thrash the daylights out of him." Hopper reached down for his cane and tapped it against his shoe.

"Toe-biter, if he comes in here we'll thrash the daylights out of him."

"You can't thrash a Vampire. It has supernatural powers." Toe-biter gazed nervously at the window, then at the door, then at the popcorn bowl.

"He's not going to come at you out of the bowl, Toe-biter."

"Everywhere I rest my gaze I see him, Doctor, smiling that horrible smile."

Doctor Hopper poured more popcorn from the pan into the bowl and stirred in butter and salt. "Mantis and I have seen a great deal of the evils of this world. We've met some rotten devils, I can tell you. In a way, I'm actually eager to encounter this Vampire of yours."

"Oh, don't say that, for heaven's sake." Toe-biter sat forward anxiously and now even his head was shaking in fright.

"You're vibrating, Toe-biter."

"Well, what of it? I've looked at the devil himself."

"There are no devils. There are, however, some extremely bad characters around, fellows who'd cut your throat for a handful of popcorn."

Toe-biter let out a little whimper, and dropped his popcorn back in the bowl. "I can't eat."

"Nonsense, best thing for you."

"How can you be so calm?"

"Training."

"Why do we have to sit here? Let's get in a carriage and ride to the other end of Bugland."

"You may go if you like. I'm staying right here." Again, Doctor Hopper picked up his cane, and put it under the brim of his derby hat. Gently he pushed the hat back on his head. "But I'll tell you this, Toe-biter—if you stay, you'll be a better bug for it."

"I don't want to be a better bug." Toe-biter reached for the popcorn again, spilling some on the floor as he did so. "I'm quite content to be a coward. In fact, I think it's my natural state. A cowardly, cringing wretch."

"Don't be too hard on yourself, old boy. You've seen some nasty things. They'd shake anyone. But the way to deal with them is head on."

Toe-biter looked out the window, toward the ragged shadow of a tree through which the moon was rising. "No one is stirring in the village. They're all hiding behind locked doors."

Hopper glanced out the window. "It is a lovely night, Toe-biter. We can't let ourselves be blinded to its beauty."

"Angus was sitting here a few nights ago, just as we're sitting here. With the moonlight shining through the window." Toe-biter got up and reached for the shade, but Doctor Hopper stopped him.

"Don't pull it down. We want no surprises."

A creak sounded on the stairs. Hopper whirled around and Toe-biter let out a gasp. Hopper grabbed his cane. Toe-biter attempted to climb under the bed, but Hopper snatched him by the collar and whispered, "Beside the door. When he comes in, bite his toe."

"What if he's wearing shoes?"

"Well, bite him on the leg."

"Oh, dear, oh dear, oh dear…"

Hopper flattened himself alongside the door, with Toe-biter crouching below him. The creaking sound continued on the stairs, then sounded in the hallway. Hopper raised the cane over his head. The door opened and a tall figure stepped through. Toe-biter struck. Hopper let out a yell and dropped his cane, for Toe-biter had bitten him on the leg.

Inspector Mantis stared at them in wonder. "Gentlemen, what's going on?"

"Mantis, you might have had the decency to announce yourself. Toe-biter here has just given me a nasty nip."

"I'm terribly sorry," said Toe-biter. "I became confused."

"Oh, never mind." Hopper picked up his cane and shook it at Mantis. "You're lucky I didn't bring this down on your head, Mantis."

"I'm glad to find you so vigilant, Doctor. It will be necessary."

"Gentlemen, what's going on?"

"You've learned something?"

"I have." Mantis glanced at the popcorn bowl. "I see you have not gone hungry."

"Now is not the time for discussing popcorn," said Hopper. "What have you learned?"

"I was under the impression, Doctor, that a discussion of popcorn is always timely where you're concerned."

"Hang it all, Mantis, Toe-biter and I have been on pins and needles for hours. And I've received a nasty bite because of it."

"Forgive me. It is a serious matter. Well, then, here is what I have learned. We are indeed dealing with a Vampire—"

"No!" cried Hopper.

"—Moth," continued Mantis.

"Moth?"

"A Vampire Moth." Mantis removed the small box from his coat, and opened it. "This is the scale I picked up at Earwig's place. I made positive identification of it in Professor Channing Booklouse's library."

"Good old Booklouse," said Hopper.

"His help was invaluable," said Mantis.

"But how could it be a moth?" cried Toe-biter. "Moths are sweet, harmless creatures. They live on pollen and nectar. They don't suck the life out of you."

"The Vampire Moth is one of several known killers in the Lepidoptera family," said Mantis.

Doctor Hopper took a handful of popcorn. "I've traveled a good bit and I've never seen one."

"No, the Vampire Moth comes from a far-off shore." Mantis helped himself to some popcorn too and nibbled it thoughtfully. "How this one got here is a mystery. But the shores of Bugland are open to all visitors."

"How can you two stand there eating popcorn?" asked Toe-biter, beginning to tremble again. "You act like you're at a cricket match!"

"We're preparing ourselves," said Doctor Hopper. "We're about to formulate a plan, eh Mantis?"

"Quite right, Doctor. I have with me—" He indicated a package under his arm. "—the rudiments of what I think will be a clever disguise."

"Disguising yourself, are you? An excellent idea."

"We're disguising *you*, Doctor. You shall act as bait."

"Just a moment, Mantis. I'm always the bait."

"Not always, Doctor. On occasion."

"Too many occasions, I'd say."

"Strategy has required it. Strategy requires it again." Mantis opened the package and laid out a piece of filmy blue material, cut into the shape of wings. "We need to pin this to the sleeves of your coat." Mantis brought out a handful of dried bee-stings, and with them fastened the material to Hopper's sleeves. "Yes, good, very lifelike."

Toe-biter took a step toward the door. "Well, I guess you won't be needing me anymore."

"We need you, Toe-biter, as never before." Mantis patted Toe-biter on the shoulder. "You are the very foundation of our strategy."

"What do you mean?" asked Toe-biter, unhappily.

"You will recall our assailant is tall. Doctor Hopper is short. To be an effective piece of bait, he must appear tall himself. Therefore he will ride on your shoulders."

"I can't support him. I don't have a muscle in my body." Toe-biter feigned weakness. "I'm a wretched specimen."

Mantis ignored him. "I've brought this length of black cloth in which I'll wrap the two of you. You shall appear as one body."

"I'm feeble, I tell you." Toe-biter continued his pathetic act. "A child could knock me over."

"Your finest hour has arrived, Toe-biter." Mantis pointed toward the door.

Whining and whimpering, Toe-biter descended the stairs, with Mantis and Hopper following him. At the bottom of the stairs, in

"I'm feeble, I tell you." Toe-biter continued his pathetic act.

the hallway, Mantis instructed Toe-biter to crouch down so Doctor Hopper could crawl on his shoulders.

"You'll see what a lousy idea this is," said Toe-biter. "I have weak knees."

"Down, Toe-biter."

"And a sprained ankle." But Toe-biter went down, and Doctor Hopper seated himself around Toe-biter's neck.

"Up, Toe-biter," commanded Mantis.

With a great show of difficulty, Toe-biter straightened. "I've got a twinge in my back."

"You'll be fine."

"I won't be fine."

"Doctor, are you secure?"

Doctor Hopper was struggling to stay balanced. "If Toe-biter would stop swaying—"

Mantis steadied Toe-biter. "Stay just like that."

"I'll get a crick in my neck," whimpered Toe-biter, but Mantis shook out the cloth and began wrapping it around them.

"I can't see," cried Toe-biter.

"You won't have to see. Doctor Hopper will guide you."

"I'm suffocating!"

"There is quite sufficient air." Mantis wrapped the black cloth entirely around Toe-biter, and then up around Doctor Hopper. "Lift your arms, Doctor, that's it, and now we fasten it at your collar."

"I can't breathe." The muffled voice of Toe-biter came from within the lower section of the cloth.

"You have plenty of air, Toe-biter. Just calm down. Now, Doctor, extend your arms outward."

Hopper spread his arms and the false wings opened.

"Excellent, Doctor. In the moonlight you'll be most convincing. And now, we cover you in *this.*" Mantis brought out the bottle of scent. "It is the perfume of the female Vampire Moth. She uses it to call to her mate. After you are covered in it, the Vampire Moth will come to you."

"Mantis, I don't like scent. I never use it."

"It's just for tonight, Doctor." Mantis opened the bottle, and a sweet odor filled the air. "How could one so evil create something so lovely?"

"Get on with it," cried Toe-biter from below.

"Quite right," said Mantis, and dabbed the scent on Doctor Hopper's face and neck, until the bottle was empty. "Very tempting."

"Did you have to use the entire bottle, Mantis? It's overwhelming. I feel like I might pass out."

"You should be down here," said Toe-biter.

"Gentlemen, we're ready." Mantis opened the door and held it for them. "Walk straight ahead, Toe-biter."

Toe-biter took a few hesitant steps. *"I'm completely disoriented."*

"Just keep going straight ahead. Doctor Hopper will guide you." Mantis walked alongside them for a ways. "Doctor, I suggest you walk to the edge of the village and then take the deserted road that leads out of it."

"Where will you be?"

"Not far off."

"I don't like this, Mantis. If quick hopping is required, I won't be able to perform it."

"*What about me?*" groaned Toe-biter.

"I won't attempt to minimize the dangers you face, gentlemen. You may well be fighting for your lives."

Toe-biter let out a groan and tried to turn around, but Mantis grabbed him through the cloth. "You have a date, Toe-biter."

"*With a Vampire.*"

"A Vampire Moth. There is a difference."

"*Tell that to Angus Earwig.*"

Mantis ignored Toe-biter and spoke to Doctor Hopper. "Doctor, you must remove your derby hat. You are, after all, imitating the female of the species."

Hopper handed him his derby. "I've never done this sort of thing before, Mantis. I don't know how."

"Make a fetching motion with your hands."

"A what?"

"A fetching motion."

"Don't be absurd."

"You must do your best to be seductive, Doctor. Imagine you're Miss Juliana Butterfly."

"I'll do no such thing."

"Well, bat your eyelashes flirtatiously."

"Mantis, the Vampire won't be able to see my eyelashes in the dark!"

"No, I suppose not. Can you arch your head provocatively?"

"I'll try." Hopper gave a little toss of his head.

"Excellent."

"I feel like a fool."

"And fan your wings a little, the way the painted lady does."

And who is the painted lady?"

"*Will you two stop jabbering? I'm roasting alive down here.*"

"I won't attempt to minimize the dangers you face, gentlemen.
you may well be fighting for your lives."

"Off you go then." Mantis gave them a gentle nudge, and they proceeded down the street. Mantis noted with pleasure that the scent was trailing in the air behind them. And the further they got the more they became a single figure, tall and slender, wrapped in filmy blue wings. When they reached the street lamp at the heart of the village, Mantis slipped into the shadows.

There he was unable to resist another look inside the jewelbox he had purchased. Set in black velvet was the sucking tube of a Vampire Moth. He examined it with his magnifying glass, identifying thin streaks of color. "There is still a trace of poison. Highly concentrated. Very little would instantly paralyze a bug."

Did the relic possess some hypnotic power of suggestion? Mantis was compelled to touch it, telling himself it was necessary. The texture of things sometimes gave mysterious hints pointing him toward his quarry. Very lightly, he stroked the sucking tube. Then, to his astonishment, it curled around his finger and stung him.

Even more concentrated than I thought, he said to himself as the poison swept through his veins. Then he fell to the ground. And everything went black.

"I*'m fainting down here,*" said Toe-biter.

"Don't give out, Toe-biter." Doctor Hopper peered up the dimly-lit village street, looking for signs of the Vampire.

"*Where are we?*"

"We just passed the center of the village. Remain silent."

Toe-biter shuffled along. Doctor Hopper thought this would be the time to practice his flirtatious airs. He did so, and a stinkbug stepped from the shadows of a doorway.

"Don't you smell nice." The stinkbug edged toward Doctor Hopper. "Whattya say we go for a walk? You don't mind the way I smell, do you?"

"As a matter of fact," said Doctor Hopper, attempting to speak in a high, female voice, "I do. You smell awful."

"Well, I can't help it. I'm a stinkbug."

When they reached the street lamp at the heart of the village,
Mantis slipped into the shadows.

"Please, leave me alone." Hopper did not want this oaf interfering with the strategy. "I'm a lady. And you have very bad manners."

"You think a guy that stinks the way I do is going to develop social skills?" The stinkbug gave a coarse laugh. "But sometimes I like a little company. Whattya say you and me go dancing? We'd make a great couple. Sweet and sour."

"I have an engagement." Doctor Hopper tried to urge Toe-biter along by squeezing his knees, but Toe-biter was exhausted, and struggling to catch his breath. He stopped in his tracks.

The stinkbug gave a leering smile. "If you have an engagement, why are you standing with me? I think you like me."

"Sir, I must ask you to withdraw." Hopper's eyes were watering from the smell of the stinkbug, and his nose was blocked up from inhaling the awful aroma, which was a cross between a skunk and a rotten egg. He squeezed his knees again, to get Toe-biter moving.

"Don't squeeze me."

"I didn't squeeze you," said the stinkbug. "I never touched you."

Hopper gave Toe-biter a kick, and Toe-biter responded with a kick of his own, right in the stinkbug's ankle.

"Ouch!" The stinkbug grabbed his ankle. "All I ever get is abuse."

"I'm sorry," said Hopper. "I didn't mean to kick you."

"Yes, I did," growled Toe-biter.

"Well, make up your mind," said the stinkbug, but his amorous mood was broken. "All right, I'll go stink up some other place. What do I care?"

"You should be home, behind locked doors. Aren't you afraid of the Vampire?"

"You think a Vampire would come near me? Sometimes it pays to be a stinkbug." The stinkbug withdrew into the shadows, though his aroma lingered on.

"Thank heavens," said Doctor Hopper.

"How much further do we have to go?" growled Toe-biter.

"A few more blocks, Toe-biter." Once again, Doctor Hopper

"Sir, I must ask you to withdraw."

spread his filmy blue wings. "I'm attempting to attract attention once again."

"*You're not much good at it, are you?*" said Toe-biter, snidely. His mood was foul, but he was under a good deal of stress.

"I have little experience in playing a seductress," said Doctor Hopper.

"*Well, I don't have any experience in carrying somebody around on my shoulders.*"

"Then we're both in difficult circumstances."

"*Mine are a lot more difficult.*" Toe-biter's muffled voice, buried in the black cloth, indicated a profound weariness.

"Toe-biter, I'd happily change places with you, but this is how Mantis wanted it."

"*Sure. He's your pal.*"

"Friendship had nothing to do with it. Mantis does not play favorites." Hopper spread his phony wings, trying to look alluring. "He evidently thought I have a certain natural charm."

"*I got charm,*" snarled Toe-biter.

"Certainly you do, old man."

"*I was elected Most Charming Bug in toe-biting school.*"

"I have no doubt of it."

"*Remind me to show you the plaque.*"

"Toe-biter, if we survive this, I will insist on seeing it."

"*You'll survive. I'll die of heat prostration and a broken back.*" Toe-biter's steps were erratic. He was next to giving out.

"Hang on, Toe-biter, we've reached the edge of the village."

The few lights from the village street lamps cast only a feeble glow. There were no carriages on the road, and no one on foot. "Visibility is poor, Toe-biter. We've only the moonlight to guide us."

"*I can't see anything anyway. Remember?*" Toe-biter's voice, coming from behind the black cloth, puffed out the material slightly, indicating how deep were the breaths he was taking. "*I'm completely winded. I can't go any further.*"

"A few more steps. I'm fanning my wings."

Toe-biter staggered a little further and Doctor Hopper made what he thought were alluring wing beats.

"You're choking the life out of me," said Toe-biter, in a strangled voice.

"I have to grip hard with my knees when I fan, or I lose my balance."

"Well, I'm losing consciousness."

"I must look seductive."

"Strike some kind of pose." Toe-biter was gasping for breath. *"Go lean on a tree."*

"All right, there's one to your right. Turn slowly, that's it. Now take a few steps."

Toe-biter stumbled toward the tree and Doctor Hopper leaned against it. "Is that better?"

"Yes. Just don't move."

"I need to do a bit of fanning, to spread the perfume about."

"All right, but not too much."

Doctor Hopper fanned his wings, and sang a few lines from a love song that was popular at the moment. His high-pitched voice cracked in several spots, but he felt the effect was good overall.

Then he listened, straining to hear if there were any sounds issuing from the darkness. He heard nothing except Toe-biter's wheezing. In a whisper, Hopper said, "Don't breathe so loud."

"Perhaps you'd like me to stop altogether."

Hopper continued fanning his wings as he stared up at the yellow moon. To it, he poured forth his song.

> *"They call her Lola*
> *the leaf roller,*
> *wild apple, cherry, and pine*
>
> *Lola, leaf roller*
> *will you ever be mine?*
>
> *You've rolled up my heart*
> *like you fold up a leaf.*

Lola, leaf-roller,
you're nothing but grief."

I'm rather good at this, he thought to himself.

"Try reciting poetry," said Toe-biter from below.

"I beg your pardon?"

"Or the ABCs. Anything but that horrible racket."

"Toe-biter, that's a very popular song."

"Not the way you sing it."

Doctor Hopper tried to maintain a superior air. "If it offends you—

"It does."

"Then I shall stop."

"Thank you."

"But I don't feel alluring without a little song."

"Fine."

Hopper stared out across the dark landscape in silence. The perky quality had gone out of his wing fanning. How was a chap supposed to carry on with constant criticism from below? Toe-biter will have to beg for a song before I open my mouth again.

He looked at the shadows cast in the grass by the moonlight. A spider's web was glistening nearby. Nasty thing, that, observed the doctor. And yet so beautiful. It shines as if hung with jewels.

"What's going on?" whispered Toe-biter.

"I'm looking at a spider's web."

"Don't fall into it!"

"Don't worry. It's not spiders we're after."

"I've had friends walk into them. Never to be heard from again."

"What was that?"

"What was what?"

"I heard—the fanning of wings."

Toe-biter froze into silence. He hated every part of being out here. His back was broken, his neck was hurting, his knees were shaking, and his feet were sore. If he had to run, he wouldn't be able to. He'd collapse into a heap, and be forced to crawl, scratching at the sand with his fingertips. *"Let's get out of here."*

"Shhhhh." Doctor Hopper was poised, listening to the *swoosh swoosh* sound in the air.

Bravely, he answered it by *swoosh swoosh swooshing* his own wings, sending out the scent of his perfume. Now is when I should add a little love song, he reflected, but Toe-biter would strongly object. Harsh criticism is ruinous to artistic feeling.

To make up for lack of a love song at the appropriate moment, he put one hand over his heart, as if pining for romance.

I ought to be in the theater, he thought to himself. *Doctor Hopper's Follies.*

In the next moment, the moon was blotted out by a large figure descending in front of it, dark wings outspread.

Hopper saw a glistening pair of eyes, a frightening leer, and in the center of the Vampire's face, the shine of a sharply pointed proboscis. The sucking tube, thought Hopper, with which he sucks the life out of his victims.

The Vampire Moth embraced Hopper passionately. "Beloved, you have returned to me at last."

"Yes…I have," stammered Hopper.

"I saw your wings. I never thought I'd see them again. And I smelled your exquisite perfume. It brings back a thousand memories." He smiled and a chill ran through Hopper's spine. A similar chill was running through Toe-biter, and his knees began shaking more violently.

"Are you cold, my dear?" The Vampire took a step closer. "I can well imagine, for you are used to warmer climates. As am I."

Hopper attempted a flirtatious smile, glad that the moonlight wasn't shining full on his face, for he felt it was a feeble smile, because his lips were trembling.

"Yes, yes, you are cold," said the Vampire, with the trace of a foreign accent in his voice. "When I first came to Bugland I too was cold. But I have warmed myself with—well, with a certain drink. You know to what I allude."

Blood, thought Toe-biter, and his knees began rattling against each other.

"How violently you shake." The Vampire stared down at the trembling lower silhouette of his companion in the moonlight. "You're not afraid of me, are you? I know it's been a long time. But I'm yours entirely, your servant and your protector."

"Thank you," said Hopper, in a thin, feminine whisper.

"How charming your voice is. So fragile, as always." The Vampire had perfect manners, and his appearance was in every way that of a gentleman—top hat, black tie, tuxedo, and of course—his cape-like wings. "But this trembling of yours concerns me."

"It's nothing," said Hopper, still in a whisper.

"You are weak. I know what you need, and I'll provide it."

More blood, thought Toe-biter, fear shooting through him in every direction.

"Good heavens, you are nearly overcome," said the Vampire. "Here, take my arm."

Hopper reluctantly put his arm through that of the worst murderer in Bugland. "You're very kind."

"I'm very concerned. You are the same as I."

The way he put this—*the same as I*—gave Doctor Hopper another flutter of anxiety, this time causing his cheeks to twitch. He was as brave as the next bug, but to have his arm through that of this brute and then to make conversation—that was demanding a lot of his nerves. He'd sooner just try and take a whack at the Vampire Moth with his bare knuckles, but it would probably not prove very effective. The fellow was clearly a powerful athlete, and of course he was a natural killer.

"I am living in a ruined castle not far from here," said the Vampire. "The last residents died, quite recently." He smiled. "Perhaps you understand?"

"Yes," said Hopper, weakly, "I do."

"So now I am the owner. I can make you comfortable there."

"You are too kind."

"You are my long-lost beloved. I will nurse you back to health, with the tenderest of care. And I must add—it will not be a chore. For you are most charming to look at."

Just don't look too closely, thought Hopper.

"Let us walk then."

Oh no, thought Toe-biter. He took a few steps, with great difficulty. He'd been carrying Hopper for an hour, and he had no strength left. Collapse was near, and then—the masquerade would be finished.

"I'm concerned for you," said the Vampire. "Your trembling increases by the moment."

"I'm—all right."

"How courageous you are." The Vampire tightened his grip on Hopper's arm. "But will you be able to make it to the castle?"

"I don't know."

"You can't fly?"

"My wings—are damaged."

"How tragic. Well, I shall fly you there." The Vampire put his arm around Hopper's waist, and then, with one powerful kick he was in the air, wings outspread.

Doctor Hopper was lifted off the ground. His knees slipped loose from Toe-biter's neck, but he caught it again with his feet, and Toe-biter came off the ground too, legs thrashing. *"You're choking me!"* he cried.

"But I'm holding you lightly," said the Vampire, not troubling to look down. They were skimming over the treetops. "But don't worry. We'll soon be at the castle."

"*...strangling...I'm strangling...*" Toe-biter continued thrashing violently and finally, able to bear it no longer, he reached up under the black cloth and grabbed Hopper's ankles with his hands. With a violent tug he wrenched them loose from his neck and fell into a pond below.

The Vampire and Hopper sailed instantly higher. "What—what's happened?" The Vampire looked down at the truncated figure of his companion. "Have I torn you in half? How could this be?"

The black cloth that was wrapped around Hopper came loose and fell away, like a dead leaf. "Ah ha! Now I see." The Vampire tore off Doctor Hopper's false wings, which fell fluttering to the ground. "You have deceived me. Very nice."

Hopper struggled against the Vampire's grip. "Let go, you swine!"

"I promised to take you to my castle, for your health. And so I shall. Although I fear your health will not greatly improve." He beat strongly at the air with his wings and they sailed high above the world, toward the ragged outline of a castle.

T HE VAMPIRE landed lightly on a stone parapet, his arm wrapped tightly around Doctor Hopper's neck. "Don't struggle, or your neck will break."

He set Doctor Hopper down, and then snapped a set of chains around his ankles. "To prevent any heroic hopping," said the Vampire. "For we mustn't have any of that."

Hopper was forced to walk with shuffling footsteps down a flight of steps that led from the parapet to the interior of castle. Where is Mantis? he asked himself anxiously. Something must have gone wrong.

The staircase wound down and around, and was illuminated by fireflies held captive in small wire cages.

"Help us," they pleaded, but Hopper was unable to help himself.

"But I'm holding you lightly"

He could only shuffle down the steps in front of the Vampire, past the imploring gazes of the imprisoned fireflies.

"They're fed each day," said the Vampire. "Why do they complain? All I want is a little light from them."

"You've taken their freedom," said Hopper.

"So I have. But in turn, I protect them." The Vampire's voice was smooth, cold, reasonable. His manners were perfect, except that his guest was in chains. He led Doctor Hopper from the staircase into a long upper hallway of the castle. Here more caged fireflies burned; there were dead flowers in a vase, some family portraits, and a suit of armor from a large horned beetle. "Dead, of course," said the Vampire, with a laugh. "But his suit of armor makes a nice trophy, don't you think?"

Beyond the suit of armor was a heavy door, which the Vampire opened. He led Doctor Hopper into a large, high-ceilinged room. Large pieces of furniture were placed around a huge open fireplace, in which cold ashes lay. "We need no fire at this time of year," said the Vampire. "It is so mild out, and the air is so sweet. It put me in a romantic mood. And then I smelled your perfume. You tricked me, little grasshopper. That doesn't happen often." The Vampire smiled, almost cordially. "How do you like my castle?"

The furniture, the lamps, the mantlepiece, the walls, everything in the room was covered by a thin layer of black dust, like soot. Doctor Hopper was greatly disturbed by it, for it seemed more than physical, as if the room were declaring—this is a place of darkness.

"Don't you ever dust?" asked Hopper.

"Ah, you mean my little layer of blackness. My dead shadows."

He forced Hopper to sit in a chair facing the empty fireplace. The Vampire sat across from him, beside a dumbwaiter in the wall, which had begun to rumble. It stopped, and opened, and on it was a plate, bearing the head of a bean weevil. The Vampire put the plate on his lap and uncurled the sucking tube from the middle of his face; he inserted the tube into the weevil's head as if it were a brandy snifter and sucked its contents dry. "An after-dinner drink I've come to enjoy." He placed the plate back in the dumbwaiter, closed the dumbwaiter door, and the device rumbled down and away through the walls of the castle. "So, now we shall have a pleasant visit. Are you wondering why I haven't killed you?"

"I must be of some use to you."

"You're wearing a most unusual scent. Very rare. Where did you find it?"

Hopper thought quickly. "In my travels. I enjoy foreign lands. I bought a bottle and brought it back."

"I must be of some use to you."

"You're lying, but I expected you would." The Vampire gazed into the cold ashes of the fireplace. "You wore that perfume in order to attract me. And so you have. Are you satisfied?"

"Not entirely," said Hopper, looking down at his chains.

"It was your intention to capture me. And imprison me. Maybe even murder me." The Vampire stood, and stirred the cold ashes in the fireplace with a poker. "And I fell into your trap."

"It is I who am trapped," said Hopper.

"Quite right. I am not so easily taken. My species has certain powers, you see." The Vampire set the poker down and extended his beautiful wings. In the center of each wing was a violet eye pattern. Hopper stared at the eyes, transfixed; a profound melancholy came over him, as if the violet eyes held a secret he couldn't endure. The Vampire snapped the wings shut again. "Perhaps my false eyes really see."

Hopper slumped forward, head falling onto his chest, the energy drained out of him. With despair, he realized that everything about the Vampire was deadly. Not even Mantis could hope to match him. And so every hope was lost.

"What's wrong?" asked the Vampire. "Did you see more than you bargained for? You should have thought of that before splashing the Perfume of the Damned on yourself."

With a difficult effort, Hopper raised his head. He knew now that the Vampire was no ordinary bug, that he carried a tremendous power. "Who...are...you?"

"Let us say I'm a foreign dignitary. I'm also the last thing you'll see on this earth."

Hopper looked past him into the shadows of the room and was horrified to see someone lying there, obviously dead. The Vampire saw where he was looking and said, "Oh, that was a guest I had for supper. The servants here are lazy and haven't taken him away yet." The Vampire took a step toward Hopper. "You'll be my dessert."

Hopper looked away from the body of the dead bug. But then he was forced to gaze at the layer of black dust that covered everything, dead shadows, as the Vampire had called it. Hopper knew the entire castle was covered in it, covered with the dusty, dried remains of numberless bugs.

"This castle is very old," said the Vampire. "I am not the first of my kind to use it." He paced slowly in front of the fire, a commanding figure in his blue wing-cape—tall, graceful, with the air of a natural aristocrat used to the exercise of great power.

"Why did you come to Bugland?" asked Hopper. "Surely there was better hunting for you in your native jungle."

"I don't expect you to understand. But it was love that brought me." He stopped pacing, turned to Hopper. "She was a beautiful creature. I adored her. But she longed for adventure. On a mad impulse, she left our native land. I found a note telling me to follow her. I was detained, for which I curse myself. I never found her. I thought this evening—that you were she."

The Vampire turned toward a window of the room, his wings rustling faintly as he did so. "But you are not she. She is somewhere out there, in the vastness of this trackless world we inhabit. Where in all that vastness can I ever hope to find her? Even my considerable powers are confounded by the task."

He turned back toward Hopper. "Her beauty was not like the gaudy little glories of a butterfly, but magnificent." He extended his blue wings. "Imagine a blue much purer than this, like the sky in the desert just as the sun is setting, a blue that grows richer and deeper with each moment until the sun is extinguished. Those are her wings, and in the center of each one is an eye like the desert moon, full and white. How I could have mistaken your rags for her wings—but it was the perfume, you see. You were wearing it, and it clouded my senses." He stepped forward, until he was towering directly above Hopper. "Now, once more, where did you obtain it?"

"In my travels," said Hopper. "A foreign port. Yes, that was it, in a waterfront store, where sailors unload their treasures."

"She was a beautiful creature. I adored her."

"Again, you're lying." The Vampire gazed at Hopper, almost amused, it seemed, by his guest's invention. "You obtained that perfume somewhere in Bugland, with the purpose of trapping me." He swept his wings about him, closing himself inside them, as if to concentrate their force within himself. "And it is her perfume you're wearing. I shall never forget it. But how it was taken from her? I can't believe that you had such power. You're nothing but a grasshopper."

Do not despise the humble hopper, thought Hopper to himself.

The Vampire yanked at a velvet bell-pull that hung beside one of the firefly cages. "You're nothing but a silly fiddler, and yet you're wearing the Perfume of the Damned. It's outrageous. You, a bug without size or strength, lacking wit, having no endurance, no elegance, no grace—what irony." He straightened the immaculate white cuffs of his shirt sleeves. "She was one of the great beauties of the world, and I was her consort." As he said this, he seemed to swell with pride, and Hopper could not resist bringing him down a peg.

"But she left you."

"She was an adventuress. Can I blame her for that? For wanting to take the most from life that she could? Perhaps she was testing my resolve. Well, here I am, still pursuing her, after ages of despair. Having looked for her everywhere, I haven't given up. No, not at all. And you, little grasshopping nobody, have brought me a trace of her. What a joke!" He laughed, and the fireflies cringed in their cages at the rising pitch of his voice. He placed the point of a highly polished shoe against Hopper's chains. "I might be moved to spare your life, if you assist me."

"It does not become a gentleman to bargain for his life."

"You? A gentleman? You don't know the meaning of the word. You're a lower class bug, without breeding, title, or refinement."

"Whatever you say," responded Hopper, but his gaze at that moment was as unflinching as the Vampire's.

Suddenly, two servants entered. They were janitor ants, large ones, and powerful looking, but their fear of the Vampire was obvious.

They stood at the threshold, visibly trembling, and waited for his command.

"Remove the body," said the Vampire, pointing with indifference at the corpse.

"Yes sir," grunted the janitor ants, and together they lifted and carried out the remains of an aquatic larva, still in bathing costume. "A diptera," said the Vampire, with a scornful laugh. "He's taken his last dip, I'm afraid."

"You, sir, are a fiend. Toe-biter was right."

"Toe-biter?"

"You murdered his friend, Angus Earwig."

"I murder so many," said the Vampire, with a sigh. "I can't be expected to remember them all. Who was he?"

"A poor, retired bachelor."

"I am unmoved." The Vampire flicked a speck of dust from his wings. "I needed his blood. I have a great destiny to fullfill and all he was doing was staring at his wall. Or was he the one who was look-ing at his stamp collection? In any case, he made no mark upon the world. While I am a prince of darkness. Look at me!" The Vampire spread his wings again, showing inner folds of iridescent red beau-ty. "There is your Angus Earwig, and the others, there in my wings. They fed the glory of my flight. They are part of my greatness."

"I'm sure they'd prefer their own poor lives," said Hopper.

The Vampire snapped his wings closed. "I must find my beloved. Where did you get her perfume? Tell me, and I'll share with you the secret of the dead shadows." He gestured toward the layer of black dust that covered everything in the room. "The dead shadows know many things."

"I have no need of such knowledge."

The Vampire leapt at Hopper, and with a single yank, snapped him to his feet. "Tell me, little grasshopper. Where is she?"

The light from the firefly cages illuminated the curls of the slen-der sucking organ with which the fiend drained the life blood of his victims. It uncurled like a spring and the tip of it touched Hopper's neck. "I have merely to inject you once. My venom is deadly."

"I hold no great store by my life," said Hopper.

The Vampire shook Hopper violently; the deadly tube made tiny sucking noises, as if eager to dine. "My offer is withdrawn. You die, now."

Finished, thought Hopper. And he thought of Miss Juliana Butterfly, and other charming young ladies to whose aid he had come at one time or another. Now, ladies, farewell. Howard Hopper shall hop no more.

The deadly sucking tube snapped in the air, then streaked toward his neck, only to suddenly twitch away. "What is that disgusting smell?" snarled the Vampire. "Is it coming from you?"

Hopper's nose was twitching too. The smell, while disgusting, was familiar to him.

"No," said the Vampire, "it's not you." He flung Hopper aside, and yanked open the door to the hallway, where one of his janitor ants cowered.

"Yes, sir?" stammered the terrified ant.

"What is that smell, you wretch?"

"I don't know, sir…"

"Is someone decomposing in the hall?"

"No, sir." The ant was crouching as low as he could, to avoid a deadly blow.

The Vampire spun around. His antennas twitched at the air. "It's not coming from the hall. It's coming from there."

He pointed at the empty fireplace. The Vampire rushed toward it, just as the head of the stinkbug appeared in the chimney, upside-down.

The Vampire stopped, with the edge of one wing wrapped across his nose, to protect against the vile smell. The odor emanating from the stinkbug was overwhelming, and more of him was now appearing— neck, shoulders, the collar of his tasteless shirt and gaudy tie—slowly he came down, as if he were being lowered on a rope. He appeared to be unconscious, his eyes closed and his mouth hanging dully open.

The Vampire whirled toward his janitor ant. "There's a stinkbug in my chimney!"

"Yes sir."

"Get him out at once, before I'm asphyxiated."

"Very good, sir."

Before the ant could try and remove the inverted stinkbug, there was a rumbling in the wall, from the area of the dumbwaiter. "What is this?" cried the Vampire. "I've had my supper. And dessert—" He nodded toward Hopper. "—has already been provided."

"Sir, I have…no idea," stammered the terrified ant.

"I see it's time to murder my staff," said the Vampire, striding toward the dumbwaiter. "First, a stinkbug in my chimney, and now this." He yanked open the dumbwaiter. Titus Toe-biter, pale with fear, stared at him from within it.

"What—?" The Vampire stared back in surprise. The dumbwaiter resumed its ascent and Toe-biter disappeared from sight.

The Vampire whirled back toward the crouching janitor ant. "There's an intruder in the dumbwaiter. You'll die for this."

"I'm terribly sorry, sir."

"And get that stinkbug out of here! I'm choking!" The Vampire wrapped his cape back up across his nose, and watched as the janitor ant attempted to pull the unconscious stinkbug all the way out of the chimney.

"He won't come, sir. He's…wedged in there."

"Weakling! I'll get him out." The Vampire strode angrily toward the fireplace. As he bent over the dangling stinkbug, he gagged several times. "How…can any creature emit such an odor…and live?"

He grabbed the stinkbug by the arms and yanked him down. The stinkbug tumbled out, in a cloud of soot. A piece of rope dangled from his ankle. The Vampire drew back, nauseated by the close contact with the odiferous insect. He swayed dizzily, choking as he backed away. "Get that piece of garbage out of here."

"Yes sir." The janitor ants, themselves dizzy from the stench, grabbed the stinkbug by the ankles and dragged him toward the door.

Upon opening it, they drew back with a shriek. The suit of beetle armor was walking toward them.

"The dead have come alive!" cried the ants, as the suit of beetle armor walked past them into the room.

The Vampire, still swaying dizzily, moved toward it. "The dead don't walk! Not in my castle!"

He yanked down a sword from the wall and aimed a blow at the beetle's head. The great black horns of armor countered the blow, and as they did, Doctor Hopper threw himself in front of the Vampire, entangling the Vampire's legs in his chains.

The Vampire kicked, landing a resounding blow on the doctor's chest, but the plucky Hopper held on.

"Get him!" cried Hopper. "Strike!"

The beetle suit clicked as its arm joints maneuvered. The Vampire lunged again with his sword, but owing to the clouds of stench he'd been breathing, his timing was off, and the sword strike missed. The armored beetle struck a blow of his own across the Vampire's wrist and the sword clattered to the floor. Hopper kicked it aside, and wrapped another length of chain around the Vampire's legs, though at the cost of receiving a second resounding kick, this time in the stomach. Right in the popcorn, groaned Hopper to himself as he doubled up into a ball on the floor.

The Vampire struck several fierce bare-handed blows at the beetle, and a crack appeared in the armor. The Vampire tried to insert his deadly sucking tube through the crack, but the beetle sidestepped it. They struggled across the room, Hopper dragging along beneath them, his chains still tangled with the Vampire's legs.

"You fight with some power," said the Vampire to the beetle. "You are not like the usual weaklings. Good, I enjoy a challenge."

"This is more than a challenge," said a voice from within the horned helmet. "This is your end."

"My end is in no one's hands," said the Vampire, and with a tremendous exertion, he tore the horned helmet from the beetle's head.

"Mantis!" cried Hopper, as the inspector's head was revealed.

"At your service, Doctor."

"You know each other, do you?" The Vampire gave Hopper another kick.

Right in the tea-cake, groaned Hopper.

"Hang on, Doctor. We'll bring him down."

"You think so, do you?" The Vampire laughed. "You deceive

"At your service, Doctor."

yourself." He unleashed a kick that separated him from Hopper's chains and sent the doctor crashing hard against the stone wall. Hopper tried to rise but the wind had been knocked out of him and the room was spinning. He crawled feebly toward the battle, the chains still dragging behind him.

The Vampire turned back to Mantis and struck a blow that widened the crack in the chest armor. He was on Mantis instantly, driving several more blows into the chest armor, which now split wide open. The sucking tube uncoiled, looking for soft tissue in which to insert itself.

"Watch out for that thing, Mantis," gasped Hopper.

"I see it, Doctor." Mantis worked his long arms slowly in the air, seeking a hold.

The Vampire evaded him easily, for though the armor protected Mantis, it slowed him. The inspector was forced to cast the armor aside, and it clattered to the floor.

"Well, there's not much to you, after all," said the Vampire.

"It should prove sufficient," said Mantis, his voice calm, as he stalked the Vampire's powerful form.

Doctor Hopper struggled to rise, but the weight of the chains and the pain in his stomach kept him bent over. "I'm...coming, Mantis."

"Do you think the two of you are enough?" snarled the Vampire. "I've held off dozens like you." He rushed at Mantis, and the two bugs grappled, each attempting to get a death grip on the other. Furniture was overturned, and the recumbent stinkbug was stepped upon. He moaned and appeared to wake, but seemed drugged. Both the Vampire and Mantis held their breath until they were far away from him, but neither released their grip on the other. They crashed into the wall, with Mantis pinning the Vampire's back against it. "Now, Toe-biter!" called Mantis.

The dumbwaiter opened, and Toe-biter held out a steaming cowfly steak to Mantis.

"Not that kind of steak, you fool."

"It's prime cut," said Toe-biter.

"A stake to drive into his heart," hissed Mantis.

"Sorry. Misunderstanding." The dumbwaiter closed and rumbled back down through the castle wall.

The Vampire used the miscalculation to break free of Mantis. Racing across the room, he retrieved the fallen sword. "Have you heard that swords have sworn an oath?" he asked with a smile. "To cut and to kill."

The air whistled as the sword passed through it, Mantis barely escaping the gleaming edge and no longer having armor for protection. "You can't outlast me," said the Vampire. "I have the strength of thousands."

"You shall need it," said Mantis, and indicated the window.

The Vampire spun around and saw: in the fields surrounding the castle, hundreds of torches burned, carried by the villagers. "Well," said the Vampire, "this is the sort of battle I like." He turned back toward Mantis. "One wretch like you is hardly any sport at all."

"Don't…count *me* out," said Hopper, still crawling feebly toward the Vampire.

The Vampire stepped lightly away from Hopper, and gazed at Mantis. "I have fought such numbers before. And here I am."

"This place will prove unlucky for you," said Mantis.

"You know my reason for being here."

"She is dead."

"You lie."

"Here," said Mantis, and reached inside his coat. He withdrew the long, transparent jewel case purchased from the painted lady. He tossed it toward the Vampire, who caught it, and stared down into it.

"No!"

"I'm afraid so," said Mantis.

The Vampire's face had turned pale, and his brow was creased with pain.

Mantis stepped slowly toward him. "You know what her sucking tube looked like."

"Yes," cried the Vampire, in a choking voice. "It had the tiniest little curve at the end, so delicate. I am looking at it, here."

"She was killed by an angry crowd, much like the one that awaits you outside."

The Vampire looked slowly up, his gaze meeting that of Mantis. "When did it happen?"

"Fifty years ago. Just after she came here, in fact. You had not yet arrived." Mantis's voice was surprisingly gentle. "The crowd that killed her was savage. They took souvenirs. What you hold in your hand is one of them, as was her perfume."

The Vampire looked back down into the transparent jewel case, where the dried sucking tube lay, on white satin. "Then it's over," he said softly.

"You should never have come to this land," said Mantis.

"Or any land!" The Vampire spread his wings with a cry of pain so deep it made the fireflies dim their lights, as if in pity.

He raced to the window, and hurled it open.

"I'm coming," he said, toward the silver curve of the moon, as if he were calling to one who waited invisibly beyond it. He leapt through the window, and spread his cape-like wings. They caught the air, and he hovered far above the ground, fanning slowly and gazing around the night sky, drinking in every detail of it. A roar came from the

"I'm coming," he said.

villagers, as they shook their torches at him. And then, from every corner of the sky, as if a thousand more stars had suddenly appeared, a flight of fireflies surrounded him. Behind them came a squadron of angry wasps who dove in at him, and stung him, one by one.

"Do your worst!" he cried, making no attempt to fight back. Instead, with wings spread, he exposed his chest to their poisonous barbs. They struck without mercy, and his great wings beat more and more slowly, until finally he folded them around himself and fell into the crowd below.

They too took souvenirs.

"HE WAS A NOBLE CREATURE in his own way," said Mantis, "but such monstrous nobility is not for this world of ours."

"I won't miss him," said Hopper, whose ribs were still aching from the kicking he'd taken.

"No," said Mantis, "there is only one creature who would have missed him. Let us hope they have found each other in some dimension beyond this one." He looked up into the bright midday sky, a tiny image of the sun and clouds reflected in his coldly glistening eyes. "In some place we cannot see, perhaps."

"This is not like you, Mantis. Very unscientific."

"Yes, I suppose it is," said Mantis, and to avoid any further embarrassment, abruptly changed the subject. "Forgive me, Hopper, for endangering your life. After setting you out as bait, I made a dreadful error. Blame it on my scientific curiosity. I examined the antique proboscis too closely. A drop of its venom touched me and rendered me unconscious. Imagine my horror when I woke to find you being carried away in the air and I could not make a move to help you."

"Tut, tut, my dear fellow, these are the risks one runs when offering oneself up as bait."

"When I regained my mobility, I rallied the villagers. Then, knowing I needed a diversion while I got into the beetle armor, I drugged our friend the stinkbug and lowered him down the chimney."

"Well, I'm glad of it," said Hopper, "for it saved my skin. And he seems no worse for it."

They nodded toward the stinkbug, who was enjoying a modest celebrity in the village square, for his part in the defeat of the Vampire. A circle of admirers had gathered around him to hear his account of the part he'd played, though they maintained a necessary distance, in order to avoid watering eyes and running noses. The stinkbug was gesturing dramatically. "I said to him, 'Vampire, you're finished.' Then I tackled him, right there in his own living room."

The villagers cheered him, and Titus Toe-biter received a number of cheers too, for he, like the stinkbug, had been giving an account of his own part in the drama. Mention of the cowfly steak was not made, only that he had risked his life going up and down in the dumbwaiter and, at a crucial moment, had come to Mantis's assistance. Some young autograph seekers surrounded him, and he obliged them, while Hopper and Mantis walked on.

"Well," said Doctor Hopper, "what have we here?"

"I believe it's the candy shop, Doctor, to which you've been leading us directly."

"A bit of nourishment after what we've been through, Mantis. Surely you don't begrudge us that."

"Not at all, Doctor," said Mantis, and even held the door for Hopper. The little bell tinkled overhead and the two bugs stepped inside.

"Oh, there you are!" cried the honeypot. She rushed out from behind her counter and threw her arms around Doctor Hopper. "Thank you, sir, oh thank you," she said, and planted kisses on both his cheeks.

"I say, steady on," said Hopper, holding the brim of his derby hat.

"But you've saved us! We can laugh again and go about our business, and live like normal bugs." She brushed at the lapel of his coat. "Oh, look, I've gotten powdered sugar all over you."

"Quite all right," said Hopper, attempting to restore his dignity.

He was not used to being kissed by candy-makers, and there were villagers peering in through the windows.

"Now, you just pick out any candy you want, sir, and as much of it as you like. It's my treat. You too, sir." She nodded at Mantis.

Mantis selected only a single honey drop. Doctor Hopper asked for fudge, and got it, in two large bags, plus another two bags of nectar-cremes. "It's made with love, sir," said the honeypot, and attempted to give Hopper another kiss, but he was able to escape her grip.

"Thank you so much...most deeply grateful..." Hopper was backing up, toward the door. When it had closed behind them, he looked down at the two bags he held. "This is really too much candy."

"Surely not," said Mantis.

"Well, perhaps you're right," said Hopper, and the two bugs walked on, toward the railroad station and the train that would take them back to their little flat on Flea Street.

THE CASE OF THE CARNIVOROUS CATERPILLAR

INS PECTOR MANTIS rapped on the door with his pipe. He and Doctor Hopper waited. Soft footsteps were heard and the door was opened a crack. Mantis peered through it sharply. "Mr. Cone Nose?"

A frightened-looking bug peeked out. "You're Inspector Mantis?" The bug's eyes darted about nervously.

"I am, and this is my colleague, Doctor Hopper."

The door swung open wide. "I hope you're prepared for what lies ahead."

"Your note said you're troubled by ghosts."

Cone Nose led them into his living room. "I can't sleep. The ghost won't leave me alone."

Mantis pointed to red spots on the slipcovers of the couch. "I take it you're a bloodsucker?"

"I come home exhausted, blood on my nose, and some of it gets on the furniture." He paced the room nervously. "Bloodsucking is dangerous work at the best of times. I've got to be well rested, and for that a good night's sleep is essential. But no sooner do I put my head on the pillow than—" Cone Nose looked around fearfully. "—the ghost comes."

"And what does the ghost do?"

"He makes noises."

"Such as?"

"A terrible ticking sound. Tick tick tick, as if he's counting off the moments to my death."

Hopper opened his medical bag and took out his stethoscope. "If you would open your shirt, please, Cone Nose."

Cone Nose did as requested and Hopper listened. "Your heart is strong." He moved the stethoscope. "The spiracle valves are clear, the tracheole tubes are good." He put away the stethoscope. "I shouldn't worry about dying if I were you."

"The ghost is breaking me slowly. Let me show you something." He led them into his bedroom. The bed was sagging to one side, the leg broken. "It was brand-new just a month ago. The ghost snapped the leg from under me in the middle of the night. I tumbled out and took a bad fall."

Mantis bent to examine the broken leg, then looked up at Cone Nose. "You may rest easy, Cone Nose."

"How can I rest easy? The ghost broke my bed."

"A ghost did not break your bed. Your housekeeping leaves something to be desired, but in this instance it has preserved valuable information. Doctor, would you please identify these tiny pellets on the floor?"

Hopper examined them. "Frass."

"Frass?" asked Cone Nose. "What's frass? Speak plainly, I'm a plain bug."

"Worms ate your bedpost."

"And frass?"

"Think of it as fertilizer, provided by the worms," said Hopper.

"And the ghost?"

Mantis said, "The ghost and the worms who ate your bedpost are closely related."

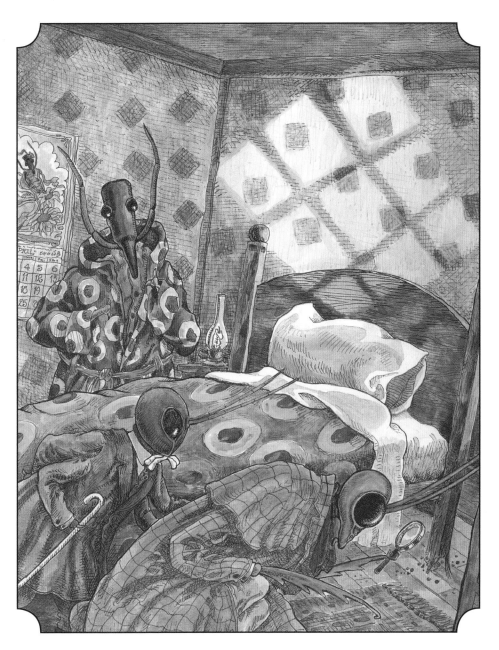

"Frass."

"I don't understand."

Before Mantis could explain, a ticking sound began. Cone Nose cried out, "There it is. The ticking of the ghost. And all you can talk about are worms."

Mantis cocked his head and said, "That is the sound of the Deathwatch beetle."

"It's coming from above," said Doctor Hopper, pointing toward the ceiling.

They hurried outside, their gaze directed at the roof.

"He's up there, the fiend," said Cone Nose.

"Not a fiend, Cone Nose," said Mantis. "Nor a ghost. It is a Deathwatch beetle calling for a mate."

"I don't hear any calling. All I hear is the terrible ticking." Cone Nose covered his ears, unable to bear it any longer.

Mantis pried the terrified bug's hands off his ears. "The Deathwatch beetle does not strum a guitar and sing beneath his beloved's window. He taps out his love call. For this he uses a sturdy piece of wood. In this case, your roof."

Cone Nose stared at the roof. "But I don't see anything. I'm telling you, it's a ghost."

"The Deathwatch beetle is hidden behind your chimney. If his love call is successful, the female will appear. He'll fly away with her and you'll be troubled no longer."

Cone Nose was not prepared to wait for this romantic interlude to come about. He shouted toward the chimney, "Get off my roof!"

"You're interfering with love, Cone Nose," said Hopper.

"And he's interfering with my sleep!" Once again Cone Nose cried out, this time shaking his fist toward the invisible invader. "Get off my roof!"

"Your effort is futile, Cone Nose," said Mantis. "The Deathwatch beetle on your roof has a strong attachment to this place."

Just then they heard wing beats coming slowly, clumsily. A shadow crossed over the roof and the wing beats stopped.

"A female beetle has answered the call," said Hopper.

Tender whispering came from behind the chimney. A moment later the Deathwatch beetles flew away, clinging to each other as they flew. "They've gone," said Mantis. "You'll be troubled by ghosts no longer."

"Well, thank heavens for that."

"But your house is falling down."

Cone Nose looked at Mantis questioningly. Mantis said, "The worms who ate your bedpost are Deathwatch larvas. Generations of them have lived in your walls, slowly eating away the timbers." He bent over in the yard, sifting a powdery material. "This is the result."

Just then there was a creaking sound, shingles fell off, and the house collapsed. The three bugs jumped back as dust rose in the air, frass flew around, and the bed of Cone Nose appeared through the broken roof rafters.

"My little house!" cried Cone Nose. "My refuge, my hideaway."

"Whatever you call it, you're fortunate not to have been inside," said Mantis. "In light of this development, I will not be presenting you with a bill for my services."

Hopper opened his medical bag. "Have a bit of fudge, Cone Nose. It's the sovereign remedy for emotional upset."

Cone Nose ate the fudge in a sort of stupor.

"Best to leave him alone," said Hopper. "The fudge will work better that way."

Mantis and Hopper walked toward their waiting carriage. But they were stopped by an official vehicle of the Bugland Police Department pulling up. Police Captain Flatfootfly stepped out. "Ah, Mantis, I've been looking all over for you."

"I'm honored by your attention, Captain."

"I haven't forgotten the small contributions you've made to my investigations in the past, Mantis." Flatfootfly looked beyond them to the rubble of shingles and roof timbers and Cone Nose contemplating it all. "Chap's house just fell down," observed Flatfootfly. "He appears to be eating fudge. An odd response."

"It's a prescribed medication," said Hopper.

"Just as you say, Doctor. I know little enough about medicine."

And even less about crime detection, thought Mantis. "Whatever your problem is, Captain, I'm sure you need no help from me. As you say, my contributions have been small." Mantis opened the door to his carriage.

"A moment please, Mantis. I've got a new case that I think will interest you."

"And the case involves—?"

"Murder, to put it simply."

Mantis removed his foot from the step of his carriage. "You have my interest, Flatfootfly."

"Then we must go to Little Biting Grove."

"The murder happened there?"

"Murders, Mantis. Several of them."

"Better and better."

"Worse and worse, if you ask me," said Captain Flatfootfly.

But Doctor Hopper understood the abrupt change in the mood of Mantis. He'd seen this change in Mantis many times. The worse the atrocity the greater was its attraction for him. Morbid? It may be the price of genius, reflected Hopper, and climbed up into the Bugland Police carriage behind Flatfootfly and Mantis.

"Ah, Mantis, I've been looking all over for you."

"LITTLE BITING GROVE is a quiet village," said Captain Flatfootfly as they stepped down from the carriage into a narrow winding street of charming little houses, each with its own garden. "But as you can see, no one is about. All of them are too frightened to go out."

"We must change that," said Mantis.

"Indeed we must," said Flatfootfly. "My superiors are growing impatient."

"But you're working with your usual penetrating methods," said Mantis. "You've already seen that soldier ahead of us is about to lose his head."

"I won't stand for any unruly behavior, not at such a critical time." Flatfootfly could see the soldier *was* swaying in an odd way. "You there!" Flatfootfly called to the soldier.

The soldier's head fell off.

"Great grasshoppers in the morning," mumbled Flatfootfly and hurried toward the headless bug.

Doctor Hopper and Mantis quickly joined him. Hopper examined the grizzly head and then the bloody neck. "The neck muscles have been chewed clean through."

Mantis pointed to a tiny hover fly above them in the air. "And no doubt, Captain Flatfootfly, you've seen the culprit."

"Surely not that creature, Mantis. It's tiny."

"Her tiny form permitted her to sneak her eggs into the folds of the soldier's neck. When the eggs hatched the larvas devoured the muscles supporting the head."

Flatfootfly hurried over to the driver of his carriage. "Summon the Dragon Patrol!"

Minutes later three uniformed dragonflies arrived, wings flashing in the sunlight. The humming sound of their wings was followed by the sound of snapping mouthparts, and the hover fly was no more.

"Swift justice," said Mantis.

"But hang it all, Mantis," said Flatfootfly, "that's not what I got you here for."

"Swift justice," said Mantis.

Hopper noticed that a ladybug was peering cautiously from behind her window curtains.

"There you have it," said Flatfootfly. "Everyone is in hiding and not because a soldier's head fell off."

Burying Beetles from the Department of Health were already arriving to cart away the decapitated soldier.

Flatfootfly continued. "I'm talking about deadly traps that have been set everywhere. Bugs have been stepping into them and now, like that ladybug hiding behind her curtain, they refuse to come out of the house."

Mantis nodded solemnly. "Can you take us to one of these traps, Flatfootfly?"

"Yes, but first I want to show you how powerful this killer can be." Flatfootfly led the way through the village to a quiet lane running through the countryside. "A perfectly peaceful landscape except for *that*." He pointed to a huge round object, spiral contours showing it to be the shell of a snail.

"A large but harmless creature," said Doctor Hopper. "It only eats plants."

"But something has eaten *it*," said Flatfootfly, rapping on the snail shell, which gave a hollow sound.

"Empty," said Hopper, peering inside it.

"Every last speck of it devoured by the killer." Flatfootfly's head was inside the shell now, his voice echoing hollowly. His head came back out. "Naturally my responsibility is not toward snails. They're huge beasts and they've got to watch out for themselves. But bugs, Mantis, bugs *are* my responsibility."

Flatfootfly led them further along the winding lane. Mantis walked beside the detective, keen eyes searching for unusual movements, things out of place, interruptions in the tranquil sounds of nature. On the waters of a pond a caddis worm was enjoying the morning floating inside a buoyant reed.

"He at least is safe," said Flatfootfly.

The caddis worm waved, and floated on. Mantis noted a shadow moving beneath the surface of the water but said nothing.

"This is what I wanted to show you," said Flatfootfly, pointing to a ragged web suspended from a tree. Hanging in it was an assortment of dead bugs. "Some late citizens of Little Biting Grove," said Flatfootfly. "And of course a web with dead bugs in it means a spider is at work. The troubling thing is, there are no spiders in this neighborhood. They were wiped out in the Spider Riots of '69. People wouldn't stand for them lurking about. Since that time no spider would dare show itself here." Flatfootfly pointed to the web. "So where is the spider who did this?"

"Where, indeed," said Mantis.

Flatfootfly removed a report from his pocket. "My constables scoured the place and no spiders were found."

Ignoring Flatfootfly's report, Mantis and Hopper examined the bodies. "They have been chewed and torn apart by their killer," said Mantis. "Yet I find no cheliceral tooth marks on these bodies nor any trace of digestive enzymes. Am I correct, Doctor?"

"Quite correct."

"And there are no traces of venom."

"Again, absolutely correct."

Flatfootfly interrupted impatiently. "I'm a simple bug, Mantis. Simple is best. Simple gets to the heart of the matter. What the devil are you two talking about?"

"Spiders inject venom into their victim. There has been no injection here."

"There are dead bodies in a web, Mantis. That's all I need to see. A spider has been at work."

"Spider fangs leave distinctive markings on the victim, like those produced by a hypodermic syringe. We find no such marks on this body. And finally, spiders cannot simply swallow the body parts of their victim. They must chew them and then squirt digestive enzymes onto them, thereby reducing them to a liquid they can easily swallow. There are no digestive enzymes left on these bodies, nor liquid traces of any kind."

Flatfootfly's head was spinning. It was always like this when he called on Mantis for help. Mantis would start talking like an encyclopedia. "And your conclusion?"

Mantis had shifted his attention to the threads of the web. "This web was not woven by a spider." He stretched one of the threads between his fingers. "Have you read my monograph, *Death by Silk*?"

Flatfootfly frowned. He never read any of Mantis's nonsense. "I skimmed it."

"Then you know that spiders spin silk of several different kinds. Some of it is used for webs, some for wrapping the victims, and some for swinging along. The silk for swinging is called, rather poetically, *gossamer*."

"This is not the time for poetry, Mantis."

"*This* silk—" Mantis snapped it between his fingers. "—is neither ampullate, nor tubiliform, nor aciniform."

"Words of one syllable would be appreciated, Mantis."

"They have been chewed and torn apart by their killer"

"It does not come from the silk glands of a spider. It comes from the mouth of a caterpillar."

"But caterpillars aren't killers!" exclaimed Flatfootfly. "They nibble on leaves. Grass and clover, that sort of thing."

"This one—" Mantis nodded toward the deadly web. "—has changed his menu."

"A carnivorous caterpillar?"

"It would appear so." Mantis held the thread up to the sun. "Instead of weaving a cocoon it wove a trap."

"What is the world coming to?" asked a disheartened Flatfootfly.

"The world has changed many times since the first bug spread its wings long ago."

"I could do without the philosophy, Mantis, if you don't mind." Flatfootfly tore at the web with his fist, freeing the dead bugs, and destroying the trap. The silk clung tenaciously to his sleeve when he tried to shake it off. "Infernal stuff..."

"Look at these, Mantis," said Doctor Hopper, plucking what appeared to be little jewels from the scraps of web that remained in place. "These are the scales from a butterfly's wings. What a dastardly crime. A butterfly has perished here."

"I'm afraid I must correct you there, Hopper. A butterfly is able to shed her scales when tangled in a web. She leaves them behind but she escapes."

"Well, that's some small comfort," said Hopper, and released the scales into the air. A breeze caught them, carrying away the little dancing bits of beauty.

As Flatfootfly struggled to get the silk off his sleeve the caddis worm appeared on the road, stripped naked. "Look what's been done to me!"

A naked worm is a shocking sight at the best of times. For Flatfootfly, whose hand was unpleasantly sticky with silk, the moment was hardly opportune. "What do you expect me to do about it?"

"You're the police, aren't you? A water beetle ripped my clothes off."

"You were floating along inside a reed. That isn't clothing."

"I'm standing here naked."

"Find another reed."

"Not as easy as it sounds," said the naked worm. "The fit must be perfect."

Hopper intervened, and addressed the worm. "Being fitted for a new reed is hardly the point. You could've been devoured by that beetle."

"But I wasn't, was I?" countered the worm, somewhat obnoxiously. "I demand action be taken."

Action was taken, but in a rather startling way. From the heart of a flower a spider leapt out and tackled the worm.

"Your report said there were no spiders in this neighborhood, Flatfootfly," said Hopper.

"Unfortunately they seem to be coming back," sighed Flatfootfly.

"I'm under attack here!" cried the worm, trying to redirect the conversation.

The spider's fangs were out and descending swiftly toward the worm's naked flesh. A powerful green arm acted with equal swiftness.

The spider was forced to release the worm and give all his considerable strength to grappling with Mantis. He managed to break away and hissed at Mantis, "This isn't over."

"I quite agree," said Mantis, calmly straightening the cuffs of his jacket. "But it soon will be."

Flatfootfly drew his pistol and fired but the spider leapt clear of the shot.

Mantis said, as if to himself, "Hydraulic pressure in the legs."

Flatfootfly was putting his pistol away in disappointment. "What did you say, Mantis?"

"His powerful jumps are produced by squeezing fluids from his body into his legs."

"I'd like to squeeze him, by the throat."

"That won't be necessary," said Mantis, who had heard a familiar hum in the air— the wings of the *pompilid*— the spider-killing wasp. She was rapidly descending. The spider spun around to meet her but the aim of the pompilid was better than Flatfootfly's. Her stinger struck the spider, paralyzing him. Then she picked the spider up and flew away.

"She will put the spider in her nest to feed her children," said Mantis.

"Pity she doesn't carry off caterpillars," said Flatfootfly. "In any case—" He pointed to the dead bodies which still had bits of silk clinging to them. "Are you quite sure this wasn't done by a spider?"

"Yes," said Hopper, "I stand by our analysis. Strange as it seems, this *is* the work of a caterpillar."

The worm wriggled upright, his naked body now covered with dust. "What about me? I was almost murdered here."

The other bugs ignored him, which greatly agitated the worm. "I get it, I'm just a worm. Somebody tries to kill me, so what?" The worm wriggled away, muttering to himself.

Flatfootfly let out a sigh and said to Hopper, "As a servant of the people I'm required to help all bugs." Flatfootfly went after the worm. "Just a minute." He took out his pocket knife, sawed off a bit of reed and slipped it down around the worm. "There."

"I'm under attack here!"

The worm examined the reed now covering him. "I don't look good in this color."

"I've done all I can for you, sir."

"I suppose it will have to do." The worm wriggled off in his new suit.

Flatfootfly returned to Mantis and Hopper. "All right, let's find this killer caterpillar."

"All caterpillars are masters of disguise," said Mantis, saying which he pointed to a bed of zinnia blossoms. Doctor Hopper poked at it with his cane. The blossoms wriggled spasmodically and one of the blossoms spoke.

"If you don't *mind*, I'm having lunch." The blossom was a harmless caterpillar whose colors matched it perfectly.

"Sorry," said Hopper.

"I go to all this trouble and *you* poke me with a stick."

"An error in judgment, old man," replied Hopper. "Consider it a comment on the effectiveness of your disguise."

The caterpillar gave a dismissive sniff, then stretched out and vanished back into the blossoms.

Hopper, Mantis, and Flatfootfly continued walking. Mantis pointed to a bird dropping.

"Nasty stuff," said Flatfootfly, stepping over it.

"I *beg* your pardon," said the bird dropping, which was another caterpillar in disguise.

"My apologies," said Flatfootfly, and they walked on. "I see what you mean, Mantis. It's not going to be easy."

"Quite right. We'll need help."

"My constables are available."

"They'll be of little use. What we require is a bouquet of tiny flowers. Preferably from the carrot family."

"I don't follow you, Mantis."

"That wasp has given me an idea." Mantis was already marching through the grass, plucking a bouquet.

Flatfootfly asked Hopper, "What the devil is he up to?"

"I'm at a loss, Flatfootfly. Footprints, clues, blood, murder weapons— that's the sort of thing that interests him. Certainly not flowers. He's indifferent to beauty. When I occasionally send flowers to an actress he mocks me."

Mantis rejoined them, carrying a large bouquet. "And now let us return to the village."

"Mantis, this is no time for courting," said Flatfootfly.

"Bear with me."

Flatfootfly had no choice. He knew he could never solve this case on his own. The three bugs returned to the village. Mantis worked his antennas until he found what he wanted— a small park at the heart of the village. It held a little bandstand surrounded by quaintly carved benches but no one was enjoying it.

"There'll be no more music in Little Biting Grove until we find the killer," said Flatfootfly, as he sat down. "I hope you know what you're doing, Mantis."

"I have the usual doubts, Flatfootfly." But Mantis held his bouquet out prominently, as if he were a suitor awaiting his beloved.

Doctor Hopper removed some fudge from his medical bag. "To quiet the nerves," he said to the others, but Mantis refused which didn't surprise Hopper. Mantis had never fully appreciated the value of fudge.

Flatfootfly had no such reservations. "Delicious, Doctor. Takes the mind off one's problems."

They sat munching their fudge, and Mantis stared off into the distance, flowers upright. In windows surrounding the park, frightened faces of bugs could be seen peering out through curtains.

Wings suddenly glistened in the surrounding foliage. A slender wasp flew into the park, her eyes fastened on Mantis's flowers. She came slowly toward him, then stopped in front of him. "Carrot blossoms, my favorite."

"For you." Mantis handed them to her.

Doctor Hopper was astounded. Never had he heard Mantis address a lady with anything but cold consideration. And here he was acting the part of the gallant bug.

"Thank you," said the wasp, her slender proboscis unrolling into the flowers from which she drank the nectar they contained. "They're very sweet and so are you."

She went slowly from flower to flower, emptying Mantis's bouquet of its ambrosia. Then she lightly tossed it aside. She looked at Mantis, her eyes glistening. "No one ever offers me flowers. They're afraid of me. Why aren't you?"

"I have the means to protect myself."

"I've heard that mantids are dangerous." She looked at Hopper. "Your little cricket friend seems helpless enough."

Hopper gripped his cane more tightly. One false move from the wasp and he'd bop her soundly. Give her something beside flowers to think about.

"But," she continued, "I'm in no mood for a quarrel. Carrot nectar always has that effect on me."

"While you're in such a mood," said Mantis, "may I ask a favor?"

"That's what this is about? You're not my admirer? I was going to give you a warm embrace."

"I admire you greatly. But just now I need something other than an embrace that could prove deadly."

She gazed at him thoughtfully, her eyes bright with predatory power. "I'm a solitary. It's best. So we won't embrace. Instead I'll grant you your favor."

"You're expert at finding caterpillars."

"I have that skill."

"Even when the caterpillars are camouflaged?"

"Especially when they're camouflaged. It amuses me to unmask them."

"I'm looking for the caterpillar who dines on other bugs," said Mantis.

"I haven't noticed him. Tell me more."

"For you." Mantis handed them to her.

"He spins a web strong enough to capture the unsuspecting."

"Some bugs just don't watch where they're going." The wasp shook her head disdainfully. "And if they can't, what business is it of yours?"

"It's *my* business," said Flatfootfly, flashing his police badge.

The wasp showed no reaction, and Hopper realized she was beyond the law. She was her own law. She was a solitary.

She turned her attention back to Mantis. "I'll find your caterpillar. And then what? Do you wish me to give him a sting?" Her little dagger seemed to twitch with anticipation.

"There's to be no stinging," said Flatfootfly. "My Dragon Patrol will accompany you and report back on the location of the caterpillar."

"I fly alone," said the wasp. "Take it or leave it."

Flatfootfly took it.

The wasp looked back at Mantis. "So for you, my little carrot flower, I go in search of your caterpillar. When I find him I'll tell you where he is." Saying which, she flew swiftly away, over the park, over the treetops.

"A most disagreeable creature," said Flatfootfly.

"Solitaries usually are," said Mantis. "I suggest we go to the village pub and await her return,"

"How will she know we're there?"

"She'll find us," said Mantis.

They walked from the park to the pub, and were greeted by the owner, a snapping bug who snapped from his seat with a little clicking sound. "Come in, gentlemen, come in." He snapped and clicked to attention in front of them. "Plenty of room." He snapped himself toward the bar which was completely empty. Only one table was occupied, by a pair of glowworms, quietly glowing in the shadowy pub as they talked.

"Curious thing, that," said Flatfootfly. "One wonders why a worm needs to light himself up."

"Much speculation has been given to the subject," said Hopper.

"*Bright Bugs of Bugland* says, and I quote, *Its use to the glowworm is debatable. Possibly it just is.*"

"It just *is?*" Flatfootfly gave a little snort of disapproval and looked at Mantis. "One of yours?"

"The author is Walking Stick, with whom I do not always see eye to eye. But on this point I agree. Many things in this world are what they are for no reason."

"Well, I don't have to like it."

"I like it no better than you do," said Mantis. He glanced at the worms. "But there they sit, glowing for no reason."

The glowworms continued chatting quietly, basking in their own light, whose secret they were not inclined to share. Let the world wonder; it was better that way.

The door to the pub opened and two of Flatfootfly's constables entered wearily. "We been everywhere, sir," said one of them to Flatfootfly. "And we can't find no spiders."

"'Cept a dead one," said the other constable.

"I know all about that dead one," said Flatfootfly.

"You're always ahead of the game, sir."

"You boys look tired. Pub-keeper, serve these bugs."

The snapping bug snapped into action, snapping out of his chair and snapping cups of nectar in front of the constables. They raised their cups to Flatfootfly. "Thanks most kindly, sir."

Flatfootfly nodded. But his mood remained foul. "We're sitting here helpless, Mantis. Waiting for a wasp. I don't like it."

"Fudge, Flatfootfly," said Hopper, offering another piece.

Flatfootfly was temporarily appeased. It was hard to munch fudge and stay upset. "But when the fudge is gone, Doctor…"

"Then we have jellybeans."

The door to the pub opened again and a distraught poppy bee entered.

"Another solitary," said Mantis, softly to Flatfootfly. "In a moment she will tell you she's been robbed."

"I've been robbed," said the solitary bee to the constables.

The constables immediately rose to their feet. "Right you are, mum. The Captain is here." They brought her to Flatfootfly. "Been robbed, sir."

"I'm not deaf, you idiot."

"Didn't mean to suggest you were, sir." The constable stepped back, eager to return to his nectar cup.

Flatfootfly turned to the bee. "Now then, miss, tell me what happened."

"My apartment was robbed. My honey is gone. They even took my wallpaper."

"Your wallpaper?"

"I worked so hard decorating the place."

"With poppy petals," said Mantis. He pointed with one of his antenna to a tiny red scrap of the flower clinging to the bee's collar.

"Yes," she said, unhappily. "I went and cut poppy petals and lined the walls with them. A lovely scarlet tapestry."

"And it's gone?" asked Flatfootfly.

"Along with my honey. Who would do such a thing?"

"A scuttle bug," said Mantis.

The bee swung toward him anxiously. "How do you know?"

"The scuttle bug steals honey and eats it."

"But why would he steal my wallpaper?"

"He is a bug without a conscience. He also eats shoe polish. He left some of it behind in your apartment and you rubbed up against it with your basket." Again Mantis pointed with an antenna. "There are traces of shoe polish on your pollen basket."

The bee looked down at the dark substance clinging to her basket. "Ugh, how disgusting."

"Its proper place is on a shoe," added Mantis, as if this might comfort her but it certainly didn't. She desperately scraped the black polish off of her basket.

"And," continued Mantis, "there is about you a faint smell of drainpipe."

Hopper intervened. "Mantis, is this necessary? Surely that remark is offensive."

Mantis clarified his analysis. "The other characteristic of the scuttle bug is his love of drainpipes. He carries the smell with him wherever he goes."

The bee made flapping motions with her wings, trying to dispel the smell. "It's not enough that he robs me," she wailed, "he covers me in his vile odor."

"Strictly speaking, it's not his odor but that of the drainpipe through which he traveled," said Mantis.

"I've got to go home and shower immediately," said the distraught bee.

"I suggest you remain here awhile longer in order to reclaim your honey," said Mantis.

Flatfootfly quickly queried him. "You know where it is?"

"The scuttle bug flies close to the ground. It gives him an easily recognizable appearance, as if he were scuttling along. He can't have gotten far. Send out these constables. Have them check the drainpipes first."

Flatfootfly barked at his constables. "Go!"

They left their nectar cups unfinished and hurried out the door.

The bee looked at Mantis. "Who are you, sir?"

"Your servant." He bowed his head slightly.

"Will they also find my wallpaper?"

"I'm afraid it will smell like a drain pipe. You shall have to cut more poppy petals."

"They're past their peak."

"Alas, I cannot resuscitate flowers."

"No, of course not," said the bee. "Well, I shall just have to use roses."

"And I'm sure they'll do very nicely," said Hopper. "May I offer you a jellybean?"

The bee's face brightened. "I *do* love a sweet." She took a dainty bite of the jellybean. "Why, it's homemade."

Hopper looked at her approvingly. She understood sweets.

She said, "You should try my honey."

"I'd be honored."

"If it's ever returned to me," she added, sadly.

The door opened and a heavy smell of drainpipes blew into the room.

"I'm innocent," exclaimed a high pitched voice.

The scuttle bug was shoved into the pub by the constables.

"If you're innocent," said Flatfootfly, "why are you carrying two pots of honey?"

The scuttle bug looked at the honeypots, as if surprised to see them at the ends of his arms. Close observation revealed shoe polish on his head. Flatfootfly said, "Put down those honeypots."

The scuttle bug set them down. "There you are," he said, as if pleased with his performance. "Not a drop spilled."

"Take him away," said Flatfootfly.

"One second, please, I beg you." The scuttle bug looked at the poppy bee. "I did it. I stole your honey. I admit it. But I wasn't always this way." He put on a pathetic face and said, "I used to just stick to drainpipes. Nothing wrong with that, drainpipes are public. I'd scuttle along in there, a bug in his proper place. Then one fateful day—" Here he made another pathetic face. "—I got my first taste of honey. It was so delicious I had to have more. It wasn't my fault, they shouldn't be allowed to make such sweet things."

"Take him away," repeated Flatfootfly.

The scuttle bug appeared surprised. "You don't want to hear the rest of my touching story?"

"No," said Flatfootfly, and the constables marched the scuttle bug away.

The poppy bee gazed tenderly into her honeypots. "It's all there. Thank you, sirs."

"The Bugland Police are happy to have helped you, miss," said Flatfootfly.

She said, "You should try my honey."

She held out one of the honeypots to Flatfootfly. "Please, have some."

The snapping bug provided slices of toast to which everyone added honey. After one bite, Hopper said, "My jellybeans pale in comparison."

The honey-fest was interrupted by the door flying open again. A goldbug staggered into the pub. In a trembling voice, he said, "I'm told the police are here."

"I am the police," said Flatfootfly, wiping honey from his mustache. "How may I help you?"

"I've been mugged and robbed by a ball of dust!"

"Sir, such a thing is not possible."

"I tell you, it was a ball of dust." The goldbug sank into a chair. His normally bright golden color had become a dull yellow.

Flatfootfly *did* notice bits of dust clinging to the goldbug. He suspected the bug had imbibed too much nectar and fallen into a dust bin. The goldbug looked at him in frustration. "You don't believe me, do you?"

"Sir, you're entitled to your version of events."

"Entitled to be mugged by a ball of dust?" The goldbug tried to blow bits of dust off himself but they clung to him with a strange tenacity.

"If I might," said Mantis, stepping over to the goldbug. "You were attacked by *Reduvius personatus*, otherwise known as the Masked Hunter. He exudes a sticky substance, then covers himself with dust and lint in which he prowls about looking for victims."

Flatfootfly shouted at his constables. "Ball of dust! Find it!" He turned to the goldbug. "My apologies, sir. I was not aware this bug existed."

"Well, you should have. You're the police, aren't you?"

"Again, if I might," interjected Mantis. "Experts speculate there are some five million unknown bugs. Officer Flatfootfly cannot be expected to have knowledge of them all."

"Well, how did *you* know about this dust bug?"

"Quite by chance I'd been reading *Disguise and Subterfuge*."

"I don't know the work," said the goldbug peevishly, which was understandable as he had dust stuck to his nose, eyes, and mouth, a situation that would make anyone peevish.

As for *Disguise and Subterfuge* Hopper knew the work and knew that Mantis himself had written it. Hopper reflected to himself that though Mantis was infernally arrogant at times, especially regarding the use of fudge, at other times he was capable of a touching modesty.

Hopper opened his medical bag and said to the goldbug, "I have a solvent here that will remove the sticky stuff that's troubling you."

As Hopper administered the solvent, Flatfootfly took out his notebook and questioned the goldbug. "What is your full name, sir?"

"Guy Goldbug."

"And what was stolen from you, Mr. Goldbug?"

"All the money I had on me. But that can be replaced. What can't be replaced, what is an irreparable loss—" He stood and turned slowly before them. "What is gone forever is *my shine*. I'm not worthy of the name Goldbug."

The result of trauma, thought Hopper. He'd seen a few such cases during the Bugland Wars. After his own wound he hadn't been himself for months, the hop in his step radically weakened.

"I'm hopelessly dull," continued Guy Goldbug, looking down at his tarnished body. "I've lost my gleaming gold."

Flatfootfly tried to act sympathetic, but being a plain bug himself he thought it was a lot of fuss about nothing. "I can't do much about your shine, Mr. Goldbug. But if we catch this masked criminal within the hour, there's a good chance we'll get your money back."

"Money is just printed paper with the Emperor's head on it," said Guy Goldbug, mournfully. "But my shine is my very being."

From the next table the glowworms looked on with true sympathy. They understood.

The door swung open and the constables kicked a ball of dust into the pub. As it rolled, dust from the pub floor stuck to its body. The owner of the pub looked on with appreciation. It would save him sweeping up at closing time.

From within the dust ball two eyes peered out. Then arms and legs emerged. The dust parted around a mouth from which came the usual, "I didn't do it."

"I'm afraid you did," said Mantis, plucking a bit of lint from the Masked Hunter and matching it to the lint still clinging to Guy Goldbug. "You left it behind when you attacked this bug."

"I never saw him before."

The constables held out a handful of money. "He had this hidden on him."

"It wasn't hidden," said the Masked Hunter. "I always keep my stuff inside my dust."

"But this *isn't* your stuff," said Flatfootfly. "You nicked it off Mr. Goldbug here."

The Masked Hunter's eyes darted back and forth within his dust. He knew the game was up. Desperately, he shook himself and a cloud of dust blinded Flatfootfly and his constables. The Masked Hunter leapt over the bar, taking bits of candy wrappers, cigar ashes, and bug fuzz along with him. Again the pub owner nodded with apprecia- tion. "That bug could go somewhere in the cleaning trade," he said to himself.

The Masked Hunter ran along behind the bar, through puddles of stale bee ale and nectar, which clung to his dust and slowed his prog- ress. By the time he reached the back door he was a sodden mess. A long green arm closed on him and squeezed him like a sponge. Bee ale and nectar flowed from him, re-creating puddles on the floor.

"That's quite enough for today," said Mantis, dragging the soggy dust ball back toward the constables, who promptly shackled him.

He shuffled away, picking up a few last bits of dust from the pub floor. The owner snapped across the floor and landed alongside him. "When you get out of jail, come and see me."

"What for?"

The dust parted around a mouth from which came the usual, "I didn't do it."

"I'll hire you to do cleanup. You're the best dust mop I've ever seen."

The Masked Hunter looked at him scornfully. "When I pick up dust, it's for a higher purpose." Saying which, he continued shuffling away, dusting the threshold as he did so.

"A soul wedded to crime," observed Mantis.

Flatfootfly turned to Guy Goldbug. "Here is your money, sir."

"Yes, thank you," said Goldbug, listlessly.

Doctor Hopper opened his medical bag again. "This is specially prepared fudge, Goldbug. Take it every day until your shine returns."

"You think it will work?"

"I've never known it to fail." Hopper snapped his bag closed with authority.

And now the door opened once more and this time a most imposing figure entered. Flatfootfly sprang to attention.

"Stand easy, Flatfootfly," said Police Commissioner Bristletail.

The Commissioner walked slowly to the bar and said, "Keeper, nectar all around."

"Right you are, sir. Coming up."

The Police Commissioner raised his glass to Flatfootfly. "I was in the neighborhood and just spoke to your constables. Very impressive work, Flatfootfly. Two cases solved and you never left this room."

"Just doing my duty, sir."

Police Commissioner Bristletail turned toward Mantis. "I see the would-be detective has joined us. What part did you play in this, Mantis?"

"None whatsoever, Commissioner. Like you I was just passing through. Captain Flatfootfly has done all the detection work."

"It's always best when amateurs leave it to the professionals." Bristletail returned his attention to Flatfootfly. "And this multiple murder business here in the village? What sort of progress are you making on that?"

"I've identified the culprit, sir. Carnivorous caterpillar."

"Never heard of one before. You're certain?"

"Absolutely."

"Bugland is a place of surprises, not all of them pleasant." The Police Commissioner finished his cup of nectar and set it back down on the bar. "Well, what's being done about this carnivorous caterpillar?"

"Awaiting the arrival of an informant, sir."

A humming sound was heard, the door swung open, and the wasp buzzed in. She met the gaze of Bristletail. Though he was one of the most powerful bugs in Bugland, she appeared unimpressed. Filled with venom, fearing no one, she smiled at him coldly. "The big bug himself," she said.

"Big enough, madam," said Bristletail, smiling with equal coldness.

"This is the informant we've been waiting for," said Flatfootfly, hurrying over to her. "You found the carnivorous caterpillar?"

"Of course I did. There's not a caterpillar alive who can hide from me." She held out a strand of silk to Mantis. "A souvenir for you. He's already spinning another web."

As Mantis examined it, his face filled with alarm. "We may be too late. Where is he?"

"I'll take you to him. But can you keep up with me?"

Police Commissioner Bristletail said, "My carriage is outside. We'll keep up with you."

The wasp flew through the doorway and the others hurried after her, jumping into Bristletail's carriage. The chase was on. Doctor Hopper, sitting beside Mantis, asked quietly, "What did you see in the silk?"

"There was a change in the texture."

"Indicating?"

"It may be too late for justice to be served." Mantis was gazing anxiously out the window, following the flight of the wasp. Police Commissioner Bristletail shouted at his driver to go faster. The carriage bounced over the country road, the driver working the reins while keeping his eye on the wasp as she buzzed on ahead of them, skimming the tops of the flowers. When she dove down behind some bushes he pulled off the road and halted the carriage beside her.

The doors opened and the passengers climbed down. The wasp led them into the foliage. Mantis, with his long stride, was right behind her. She stopped suddenly and pointed to the underside of a leaf, a strange smile on her face.

"We're too late," said Mantis.

Clinging to the leaf was a cocoon of silk.

Police Commissioner Bristletail said, in frustration, "Cocoons and pupas can't be touched. I didn't make the law, and I don't like it, but there it is."

By weaving a web around himself, the carnivorous caterpillar had put himself beyond the law. Now safe inside his cocoon, his old body was being dissolved, undergoing partial death, turning into a kind of soup from which a new body would be formed.

"All his crimes are behind him now," said Mantis.

Police Commissioner Bristletail shook his head ruefully. "What's the killer going to be when he comes out?"

"He will emerge as a drab little moth who lives only on nectar." Mantis inserted into his wallet the strand of silk the wasp had given him. He would put it with souvenirs of other cases.

They all gazed at the cocoon, in which the most sacred mystery of Bugland was being celebrated. "Does he dream of the murders he has committed?" asked Mantis of no one in particular.

"I'd like to give him something to dream about," said Flatfootfly. "If I had my way we'd rip the thing down."

"No good, Flatfootfly," said Police Commissioner Bristletail. "The law is quite clear on the sanctity of cocoons. This case is closed, now and forever."

They walked back to the carriage and climbed in.

The wasp flew into the air, putting events quickly behind her. The brief interlude with the earthbound bugs below meant nothing now; the rays of the sun gave her direction and a purpose that was hers alone. She felt the glory of her wings and the magic of her freedom.

Bristletail's carriage carried its passengers back to the capital of

"All his crimes are behind him now," said Mantis.

Bugland, and found its way to the little flat on Flea Street where Mantis and Doctor Hopper had their rooms. Bristletail said, "I hope, Mantis, you've learned something from the way Captain Flatfootfly handled the case."

"I certainly did. I always do."

And Flatfootfly, who visited them on Flea Street when certain cases drove him to desperation, said, "Give my best to Mrs. Inchworm. She spreads a lovely tea."

"I'll do that, Flatfootfly." Mantis closed the carriage door and Bristletail rapped with his cane, signaling the driver to move on. He watched Mantis walk up the lane toward Mrs. Inchworm's house. "I've seen him box at the Bugland Charity Matches. Packs quite a punch."

"Yes, sir," said Flatfootfly, "he knows how to handle himself."

"Knows nothing about the crime game, of course."

"As you say, sir."

And the police carriage rolled on toward Bugland Yard.

IN THE LITTLE FLAT on Flea Street, Doctor Hopper was preparing a new batch of fudge.

Mantis added the strand of carnivorous caterpillar silk to his collection. "Occasionally I am outwitted. It brings with it a certain sting to my self-esteem."

"Happens to the best of us, Mantis. Don't take it too hard."

"Holometabolism, Doctor." Mantis laid a thin transparent membrane over the strand of silk as he fastened it into his album.

"Eh?"

"The transformation of a caterpillar into a moth."

"Oh, yes, quite. Studied the process in medical school. The moth emerges from the pupa at dawn. Rather nice, that. Steps out into the morning sunlight totally transformed. Of course the process is completely automatic." He stirred the concoction in his mixing bowl, then poured the mixture into a double boiler. "But turning chocolate,

"Happens to the best of us, Mantis. Don't take it too hard."

butter, heavy cream, vanilla and powdered sugar into fudge—that requires a special act of concentration."

He checked the temperature carefully. It was now 240 degrees. "At this point, it must not be stirred. If it is, all is lost."

There was a tap on the door and Mrs. Inchworm entered. She was carrying an envelope. "For you, Mr. Mantis."

Mantis opened the envelope. "From Flatfootfly. Two tickets to the Bugland Follies."

IN HIS HOUSE in Little Biting Grove, Guy Goldbug stopped suddenly in front of the mirror and peered closely at his reflection. "Can it be...?"

He turned left and right, examining the leathery shell over his abdomen. Little sparkles of gold were appearing. He hurriedly downed another fudge pill. The sparkles increased in number, finally coalescing into a uniform iridescence that covered him completely.

Goldbug spun around in front of the mirror, then hurried to the door, threw it open, and shouted into the street. "My shine has come back!"

"That's nice," said the ladybug next-door. She no longer hid behind her curtains. She was once again working happily in her garden.

Goldbug ran down the street, waving his arms. "My shine has come back!"

"Congratulations," said the glowworms walking along arm in arm.

"Fudge!" cried Goldbug.

Not everyone understood what he meant by this but the villagers were pleased to see Goldbug shining again. It was yet another sign that everything in the sleepy village of Little Biting Grove had come back to normal.

And in the cocoon outside the village, another dream was unfolding. Of a shadowy past? Or a brilliant future? Only the dreamer can know.

Or perhaps not even the dreamer.

THE CASE OF THE MEALYBUG DIAMONDS

THE LITTLE FLAT on Flea Street was quiet, except for Doctor Hopper's gentle snoring. Once again, he'd eaten an entire pan of fudge, and it had put him directly to sleep.

In another corner of the room, Inspector Mantis sat over his chessboard, staring down at the pieces. He was playing a game of chess by mail with an old friend, Quentin Sucking Louse, a devious and masterly player. Sucking Louse's move was inscribed in his latest letter to Mantis, which the Inspector had just read, and was now executing. "Hmmmmmn, Queen Bee to Drone Four, you're a clever devil, S.L."

Mantis, engrossed in dealing with Sucking Louse's masterly move, grew unconscious of all else around him. However, Doctor Hopper, though deep asleep and filled with fudge, felt a rustling of the thread-like hairs on the appendages at the end of his abdomen, tiny hairs which could pick up the faintest of ground vibrations, and were now alert to the closer and much heavier tread of a footstep on the stairs.

"Mantis, someone's coming."

"Right you are, Doctor." Mantis rose from his game, walked to the door and opened it. A large beetle stood in the doorway, clutching a bouquet of flowers in one hand and a box of chocolates in the other.

"I hope you like these," said the beetle, with a courteous bow, and handed the flowers to Mantis.

"To what do I owe this gesture?" asked Mantis.

"And here are some chocolates for your associate, Doctor Hopper. His taste for sweets is well-known."

"Why," said Hopper, getting up from his chair, "that's most decent of you, Mr...Mr..."

"Pleasant Beetle. Cedric Pleasant Beetle." Cedric Pleasant Beetle looked around the room. "What a lovely flat this is, so charming, so well-appointed. And you two gentlemen are looking extremely well, I must say. Is there any little thing I can do for you?"

"It's most pleasant of you to offer, Pleasant Beetle," said Mantis, "but it is we who must be of service to you, I think."

"Yes, quite. My pleasantness does make for delays in getting to the point, doesn't it. But we Pleasant Beetles aim to please, above all else. My, what a charming view. Allow me to compliment you on it. Oh, and what an excellent carpet that is. I must say you have good taste."

"Pleasant Beetle, if you would come to the point," said Mantis, impatiently.

"Yes, yes, forgive me, I'm being overly pleasant. I say, what a charming aroma of fudge there is in this room. Every room should smell just like this one. Such a pleasant smell—oh sorry, I was doing it again, wasn't I?"

"Sit down, Pleasant Beetle," said Doctor Hopper. He opened the box of candy and set it on the table between them.

"Doctor," said Mantis, "you've just eaten an entire pan of fudge. Surely you have no room left for candy."

"You're wrong, Mantis, I'm happy to say." The doctor helped

"I hope you like these"

himself to a chocolate nougat, and bit into it happily. "Very fine quality, Pleasant Beetle."

"I'm so pleased. You know how to enjoy life, Doctor, I can see that. You have a gleam in your eye and a lilt in your voice. It's such a pleasure to meet someone like you."

"Pleasant Beetle," growled Mantis.

"Ah yes, quite. Being pleasant again. Difficult habit to break, you see, but why would one want to, really, for it is so extremely pleasant to be pleasant. Well, then, I'll try to come to the point."

"That would be most gratifying," said Mantis, gazing at Pleasant Beetle intently.

"There's been a terrible scandal. One which promises to ruin a very decent young gentleman."

"Now," said Mantis eagerly, "we're getting somewhere."

"You are aware of the achievements of Colonel Lucas Mealybug?"

"Twice decorated for bravery in the Great Bugland Wars, later made ambassador to Tomatopatch, where he was of inestimable service to the Intelligence Service. Retired to his country home in Old Wormy Grape, Seedpod-on-Stem. There he tends a very elaborate garden. Family colors are blue and green, on a crest whose principal inscription is, I believe, Honor Before All. Beside that I know nothing." Mantis was leaning forward in his chair now, his eyes glistening with interest. His knowledge of the families of Bugland never failed to astonish Doctor Hopper, who was trying to shake off a fudgy drowsiness and contribute something useful to the conversation.

"Well," continued Pleasant Beetle, "his son, Miles Mealybug, has been making a complete fool of himself."

"Pray, give me the particulars," said Mantis, as he brought his long elegant fingertips together in an attitude of keen concentration.

"Young Mealybug has fallen in love with someone his family deems most unsuitable."

"And she is?"

"Miss Allegra Warblefly."

"Now," said Mantis eagerly, "we're getting somewhere."

"The music hall singer!" Doctor Hopper came upright in his chair. "A delightful creature. Have you heard her, Mantis?"

"Attendance at the music hall is not one of my pastimes, Doctor, and I'm surprised to learn it is one of yours."

"Come now, Mantis, don't be so pompous."

Mantis ignored this barb, and returned his gaze to Pleasant Beetle. "Forgive us, Pleasant Beetle. You were saying?"

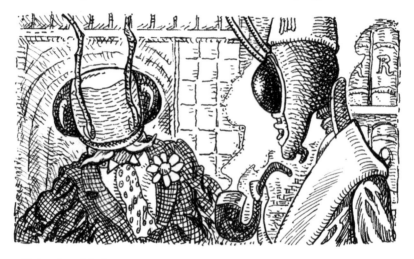

"Miss Warblefly is a nice enough young person, in fact I might say she's perfectly charming and indeed extremely pleasant looking as well as sparkling in her conversation. And as for her singing, she is considered quite gifted. Her manners too are most pleasing. I have only pleasant things to say about her, you see, and—"

"Pleasant Beetle," growled Mantis again.

"Oh, sorry. Doing it, wasn't I. Well, pleasing as she is, she's just a little nobody as far as Colonel and Mrs. Mealybug are concerned. They've been much upset by their son's behavior. To make matters worse, Miles has been giving Miss Warblefly gifts he can ill-afford. He has not come into his inheritance yet, and his spending money is gone. So, he has taken to pinching some of the family jewels for Miss Warblefly."

"A piece of folly, certainly," said Mantis, "but this situation is hardly beyond the powers of Colonel Mealybug to solve. He will act swiftly to see that the jewels are returned to the family. I'm sorry, Pleasant Beetle, but what you've described is a purely domestic affair and not something I am interested in."

"Please," said Pleasant Beetle, "let me finish."

"By all means," said Mantis, but his gaze had returned to his chessboard and the problem sent to him by Quentin Sucking Louse.

"Miles Mealybug took a priceless diamond necklace of his great-grandmother's and gave it to Miss Warblefly."

"I'm sure it looks beautiful on her," said Doctor Hopper, which earned him a disapproving frown from Mantis. "Sorry," said Hopper. "Most inappropriate remark. Fudge, you know. A magnificent food, but too much clouds the thinking."

"Well," said Pleasant Beetle, "Miles Mealybug realized he'd gone too far. He went to the theater where Miss Warblefly performs and explained the situation to her, whereupon she burst into tears. For the necklace had been stolen that very afternoon."

"Ah ha!" Mantis spun around from his chessboard.

"And this is where you come in, Mantis. If the police are summoned, the matter will get into the press and young Mealybug's future will be wrecked. He's being groomed for the diplomatic corps, you see."

"I fear he has much to learn about diplomacy," said Mantis.

Pleasant Beetle nodded. "You're right, of course. But, please, say you'll help him."

Mantis turned toward Hopper. "Well, Doctor, it seems as if I am to attend the music hall, after all."

"And much good it will do you, Mantis," said Hopper. "Miss Warblefly has the voice of an angel."

"Does she?" remarked Mantis, absently, as he slipped his magnifying glass into his coat pocket.

"Yes," said Doctor Hopper, a dreamy look coming into his eyes. "I understand that dozens of chaps are mad about her."

"Anyone we know?" asked Mantis, with a taunting sidelong glance.

"I couldn't say." Hopper wrapped a few chocolates in a napkin and slipped them into his pocket. The evening could prove to be a long one, and provisions might run out.

"I suggest you take your stoutest walking stick, Doctor. You may need to defend yourself."

Pleasant Beetle cringed. "Surely that won't be necessary."

"We do not know with whom, or what, we are dealing," said Mantis. "We'd best be prepared."

A CARRIAGE DRAWN by a stout pair of horseflies drew up at the Royal Monarch Music Hall on Cultivated Pea Street, and Mantis, Hopper, and Pleasant Beetle stepped down, into the bustling theater crowd. "I have box seat tickets," said Pleasant Beetle, and led the way into the theater. The lobby was crowded with bugs from every level of society. Most conspicuous were a number of dashing young dandyflies. "Shallow fellows," said Hopper.

"You know them, Doctor?" asked Mantis.

"They are among Miss Warblefly's suitors. They usually manage to get into her dressing room after the show ends. Any of them could have stolen the necklace, and I wouldn't put it past them."

Mantis eyed them carefully, but passed them without a word. Pleasant Beetle led the way upstairs to the box seats. "I hope these will please you, gentlemen," he said, as he opened the door to their box.

"Why, they're the best seats in the house," said Doctor Hopper, whose usual seat was the last row of the balcony, where he could eat popcorn without disturbing anyone. He would forego popcorn tonight, as Mantis wouldn't approve of the crunching.

"I'm pleased that you're pleased," said Pleasant Beetle, as they settled into the comfy seats. "But is there anything I can do to make it even more pleasant? We Pleasant Beetles aren't happy until everyone is completely satisfied with the pleasantries."

Dare I request popcorn? wondered Hopper.

But before the problem could be resolved, the orchestra took their seats and the curtain went up. A team of tumblebugs came out, and tumbled around with great strength and dexterity as the crowd cheered.

"There you are, Mantis," said Hopper, "see what you've been missing? There's nothing like a good bit of tumbling."

"Fascinating," said Mantis, with boredom in every syllable.

"He's very hard to please," whispered Hopper to Pleasant Beetle.

An anxious look came over Pleasant Beetle's face. "Why, that's awful."

"Not your fault, Pleasant Beetle," said Hopper. "He's a brilliant thinker, but stiff as a poker when it comes to fun."

Pleasant Beetle's evening might have been ruined had not Miss Warblefly appeared on stage at that moment. She was so lovely, and her voice so exquisite that Pleasant Beetle could only melt along with the other gentlemen in the audience. Mantis alone seemed unmoved. His gaze was riveted to her, nonetheless, with an icy coldness.

She sang many of the old favorites that night—Glow Worm, Bug of My Heart, and others. She strolled the stage as she sang, twirling a parasol and performing small, charming dance steps.

Someone tossed a rose and she picked it up and gestured with it as she sang, then tossed it gently back over the footlights, to the delight of the dandyfly who leapt from his seat to catch it. When Miss Warblefly finished her act, they called for more, and she sang Stung By You and My Gypsy Moth. Many other acts followed hers, but when the evening was done, it was she the audience called for, and a dozen bouquets were thrown at her. When the final curtain closed, Pleasant Beetle led the way backstage to her dressing room. It was surrounded by admiring dandyflies waiting to get in. They were extravagantly attired, postured pretentiously, seemed jealous of each other, and snubbed Pleasant Beetle as he smiled at them warmly. "What a pleasant group," he said, turning to Hopper. "They've all had a good time, everyone is pleased as can be, and what could be better than that?"

"Pleasant Beetle," said Hopper, "your ability to always think well of your fellow bug is admirable."

"Nothing to it, really. My, what a brightly pleasing star on this dressing room door. Catches the light nicely, don't you think?"

"Get on with it, Pleasant Beetle," said Mantis.

"Certainly." Pleasant Beetle knocked. "Miss Warblefly, it is I, Pleasant Beetle. I've brought Inspector Mantis and Doctor Hopper."

Miss Warblefly opened the door and all the dandyflies began to call to her.

She strolled the stage as she sang

"Allegra, my darling!"

"It is I, my dearest!"

Miss Warblefly threw kisses to the clamoring dandyflies and then motioned Pleasant Beetle to come in with his guests. The three bugs entered the dressing room. Doctor Hopper, with great pleasure, shut the door on the dandyflies. Then he turned, and his heart became a piece of melting chocolate. Allegra Warblefly was even more beautiful up close, and he vowed to move heaven and earth to help her out of the predicament she was in. "Doctor Howard Hopper at your service," he said, bowing low to her.

"And I am Inspector Mantis." The detective was already casting his gaze around the room. "You have recently been visited by a vinegar fly, have you not?"

"Why, yes," answered the astonished Miss Warblefly. "How did you know?"

"A faint smell of ethyl acetate of alcohol lingers in the air. And what was the vinegar fly's business here, if I may ask?"

"He wished an autograph. I obliged him."

"No doubt the fellow was drunk?"

Miss Warblefly reddened. "Yes, he seemed a little unsteady."

Mantis turned to Hopper and Pleasant Beetle. "The vinegar fly lives in wine cellars. Tipsy most of the time as a result." Mantis turned back to Miss Warblefly. "Under the circumstances, I think you might consider setting your dressing room off limits to the public."

"But I couldn't do that. You hear them out there—" She nodded toward the closed door, through which the calls of the dandyflies still came.

"Allegra, one glance is all I ask!"

"Don't shut us out like this, dear lady!"

"I can only advise you," said Mantis, and whirled in the other direction, his magnifying glass out, his keen eyes continuing their investigation of the room. The intensity of his purpose rendered the others silent, a silence that was only broken by the arrival of young Miles Mealybug.

"Oh Miles," cried Miss Warblefly, as he entered the dressing room, "thank goodness you're here." And she sobbed openly, and threw herself into his arms.

"There, there, Allegra, don't cry," said young Mealybug. "I'll straighten out this whole wretched mess."

"Your intentions are laudable," said Mantis, as he touched at something in the upper corner of the room, "but I believe this matter is beyond your grasp."

"Never!" Miles Mealybug stuck his chin out pugnaciously. "No suspicion must ever fall on Allegra. I would gladly die for her."

"That won't be necessary." Mantis turned to young Mealybug, over whom he towered. "But be so good as to run your finger along the edge of that crack in the ceiling."

Mealybug, much puzzled, did so, and to his astonishment, his finger struck there. "Why, I'm—"

"Glued," said Mantis. "A parasitic glue worm was in here, gentlemen, and I cannot believe it was to collect an autograph."

"I saw no such creature," said Miss Warblefly.

"He was hidden on the ceiling, Miss Warblefly, glued there by his foul secretion." Mantis turned to the others. "The glue worm is masterful in the art of camouflage."

"And it was he who stole the necklace?" cried Pleasant Beetle. "How terribly, deeply unpleasant."

"He waited until Miss Warblefly had removed her necklace. You did remove your necklace, Miss Warblefly?"

"Well, yes, when I was changing my costume."

"At that moment the glue worm lowered a sticky strand, attached it to the necklace, and reeled it in. Young Mealybug here can tell us just how sticky the glue is."

Mealybug managed to wrench his finger free. "It sticks like anything."

"When Miss Warblefly discovered the necklace was gone, she didn't think to look on the ceiling, for why would she? She hurried out to find help."

"Yes, that's just what I did," said Miss Warblefly.

"And the glue worm?" asked Doctor Hopper. "How did he escape?"

"I think you'll find a thin trail of glue goes across the ceiling to the transom over the door—"

"—and on out!" cried Hopper. "Oh, the wretch."

"It's a curious thing about the glue worm," said Mantis. "He may stick to his glue, or detach from it, as he pleases. He is perfectly suited to a life of crime, except for one little failing—he leaves a trace of his infamous glue wherever he goes."

Doctor Hopper expressed impatience here, for Mantis was capable of trotting out his erudition at precisely the moment when a fellow should get going, hot on the trail, to remove all suspicion from a lovely lady. "Let's not shilly-shally, Mantis."

"Is that what I'm doing, Doctor? Forgive me. Perhaps you would care to lead us."

"I saw no such creature"

"Right you are," said Hopper, and charged out of the dressing room, cane in hand and his eye on the thread of glue. In less than ten seconds he'd lost it. Mantis joined him in the hallway, amidst the milling dandyflies who, as soon as the door had opened, rushed toward it.

"Allegra, my precious, let us have tea!"

"Allegra, if you don't see me, I shall hurl myself against some flypaper."

Doctor Hopper looked at Mantis in frustration. "The thread of glue has vanished!"

Mantis showed no surprise. "The glue worm attached himself to someone, who carried him out of the theater."

"Then how are we to find him?" asked Hopper in exasperation.

"Doctor, I must say I enjoyed the tumblebugs. Marvelous, weren't they?"

"Tumblebugs? Mantis, have you lost your mind? This is no time for discussing tumblebugs."

"Ah, but I think it might be, Doctor. Did you know that the secretion of the glue worm stains cloth in a most unusual way?"

"No, I didn't know. How should I know? I've never formed any attachments to a glue worm. But what has that to do with tumblebugs and what do tumblebugs have to do with anything!"

"One of those excellent tumblers had a most unusual stain on his costume. Let us go and pay a visit to that distinguished family of performers, shall we?"

"Mantis, forgive me. Nothing escapes you." Doctor Hopper fell into step beside the great detective, and together they walked along the backstage hallway, beneath hanging sandbags and dangling ropes.

"Gentlemen, please, wait for me!" Pleasant Beetle caught up, just as the Singing Katydid Sisters passed from the other direction, in their bright costumes, followed by the Processionary Moths, a precision dance group. "Pleasant, most pleasant," said Pleasant Beetle, observing them go by. "There is nothing so pleasant as beauty on parade. What? Eh?"

"Steady on, Pleasant Beetle," said Doctor Hopper. "We have work to do."

"Righty-ho," said Pleasant Beetle. "Following a clue, are we?"

"Just paying our compliment to a performer," said Mantis.

"Excellent," said Pleasant Beetle. "Nothing so pleasant as compliments to a performer. Compliments all around, I always say. Can't have too many compliments."

Mantis stopped in front of a dressing room, then rapped on it with his fist. It was opened by an older Tumblebug, who was, in fact both father and leader of the Tumbling Tumblebugs. He gave Inspector Mantis a congenial smile. "What can I do for you?"

"We wish to speak to your son, sir," said Mantis.

"I've got five of the no-good little darlings. Which one's in trouble this time?"

"I believe—" Mantis squinted through the open doorway. "—yes, that one there, with the stain on the back of his shirt."

"That'd be Stumble." The father turned toward his son. "What've you been up to?"

"I'm not receiving visitors," snapped the young bug. He was seated with his brothers, playing cards.

"Ah, but you are," said Mantis, going up to him.

"Who are you?"

"I'll ask the questions," said Mantis.

"That's right," said the elder Tumblebug, and tweaked his son's antenna. "And you'll do the answering, without any smart remarks." He turned to Mantis. "They're fine athletes, sir, the best tumblers in Bugland, but they're young and stupid—"

"I ain't stupid!"

"You're stupid as an empty cocoon!" Another parental tweak on the antenna was given, and the young bug tumbled off his chair, and backflipped across the room, from where he snarled defensively at Mantis.

"Whattya want with me?"

"You carried a glue worm from Miss Warblefly's dressing room to somewhere outside this theater." Mantis was across the room in two strides of his long legs. He spun the bug around. "The stain is here—" The outline of a glue worm could be clearly seen on the back of Stumble Tumblebug's costume.

"All right, so what if I did? There's no law against it."

"Where did you deposit him?"

"I don't have to tell you. Who are you?" The young bug attempted to make a run for the door, but his father performed an astounding backflip, grazing the ceiling and landing directly in front of the door. "You're not going anywhere, lad."

"I say," said Pleasant Beetle, "that was remarkable, don't you think, gentlemen? Pleasantly spontaneous, and pleasing in grace of execution, the sort of performance we have come to readily associate with the family Tumblebug." Pleasant Beetle was doing his best to reduce the tension in the room, but no one paid him any attention. The elder Tumblebug had his son by the collar and was shaking him.

"Answer the question or I'll tumble you out of here on your head."

"I'm not receiving visitors"

"All right, all right." The young tumbler shrugged, trying to maintain his dignity. "The glue worm said he needed to give somebody the slip. Asked me to take him home. He gave me a few dollars to do it and I didn't see the harm."

"And where was home?"

"The Lacewing Hotel."

Mantis spun around and left the dressing room without another word. Doctor Hopper and Pleasant Beetle hurried to keep up with him as Mantis stepped into the street outside the theater. Their coach was waiting for them, and they climbed inside it, with Mantis calling out an address to the driver.

The doors of the coach were closed and Doctor Hopper reached into his pocket for a bit of candy. Mantis gave him a sidelong glance. "Eating again, Doctor?"

"One has to keep one's strength up, Mantis. We don't know what's ahead." He offered a chocolate to Pleasant Beetle.

"Thank you, how very pleasant. Delicious, delicious. Wherever did you get such exceptional candy?"

"You gave it to us, Pleasant Beetle. Have more. Mantis won't be wanting any."

"Most pleasant—the shape, the color, the creamy interior. I don't believe I've ever had a more pleasing piece of chocolate. Ah, life's pleasing pleasures passing pleasurably. A cab ride, a chocolate, good company—and look at the charming character of the streets..."

"They will soon lose their charm," said Mantis, and before long this was true. The bright lights of the theater district were gone, and here were only shadows. Dilapidated buildings stood at ruined angles, their doors off the hinges and their windows broken. Trash was everywhere, and few of the street lamps were working.

"Well," said Hopper, "this is certainly unwholesome."

"But nonetheless there are some pleasant little touches," said Pleasant Beetle. "I mean, it's not spoiled by being crowded."

"Yes," said Mantis, "only a lunatic would be out here at night."

"Well," said Hopper, "this is certainly unwholesome."

"And look at the bright splash of color on that door. A valiant attempt to cheer things up."

"That is blood, Pleasant Beetle," said Mantis.

"Oh dear. Is there no little sign of pleasantness at all?"

Nothing remotely pleasant could be found. An air of decay and foul play seemed to emanate from every door and window. The few figures who did appear on the street kept themselves hidden in shadow. Pleasant Beetle gave a shudder. "Most unpleasant. Makes me feel quite out of sorts."

"Hotel up ahead, gents," said the coach driver, calling down to them. "I won't be waiting for you. Too dangerous, it is."

"Silas Spittlebug," said Mantis to the driver, "don't you remember me?" The lean inspector of crime put his face into the carriage light. "You and I caught Mad Jack Stablefly, the fastest rider in Bugland."

"Not fast enough, were he! Har har!" The driver touched the brim of his hat with his whip handle. "Sorry, Inspector Mantis, I din't rec'ergnize you. I'll be waitin' here for you, sir, never you fear."

"Thank you, Silas," said Mantis, stepping down from the carriage as it pulled to a stop. "I shall make it worth your while."

"Don't worry 'bout that. It's a pleasure to serve you, it is. And if anybody tries to meddle with me, they'll get the end of my whip in their eye."

The Lacewing Hotel stood before them as they stepped down from the carriage. The entranceway was poorly lit, and broken bottles lay on the sidewalk leading up to it.

"A pretty little place," said Mantis, as they climbed a set of crumbling steps to the front door.

A vinegar fly lay across the threshold, alcoholic fumes escaping his snoring lips. "I say, Mantis," said Doctor Hopper, "could this be the same vinegar fly who's been hanging around Miss Warblefly's dressing room?"

"Very likely," said Mantis. "But the part he played was diversionary. I expect he kept Miss Warblefly's attention while the glue worm

"A pretty little place"

sneaked into her dressing room behind him." Mantis gazed down at the snoring vinegar fly. "I doubt if this fellow knew what he was doing, or why. Leave him lie where he is, for his dreams are do doubt happier than his life."

They stepped over the unconscious vinegar fly and entered the lobby of the hotel. Pleasant Beetle craned his head around in every direction, trying to find something pleasant, but again he was disappointed. The lobby held a few broken pieces of furniture on which a layer of dust had settled. A gas lamp on the wall sputtered ominously, its erratic flame causing the lobby to jump with threatening shadows. Pieces of plaster from the ceiling lay on a stained, threadbare carpet, along with damp, yellowing pages from an old Bugland Gazette, some empty nectar bottles, and a discarded shoe. Pleasant Beetle managed to say, "Yes, gentlemen, it has fallen into decay, but once it was bright, once it was new and shiny. You must say that for it. Once it breathed with the spirit of youth and joy. How pleasant it must have been."

"It was always a ruin," said Mantis, flatly.

A dagger moth sat behind the reception desk. Mantis spoke softly to his companions as they approached him. "The knife-like markings on his wings give a fairly accurate portrait of his character, I'll wager."

The dagger moth stared at them suspiciously. "There's no rooms tonight."

"In what room is Mr. Glue Worm?"

"You friends of his?"

"Old friends," smiled Mantis, and slipped a Royal Bugland banknote across the desk.

"Number 22, second floor," said the dagger moth, pocketing the money.

"Thank you so much," said Pleasant Beetle. "The warm reception you've given us is most pleasing."

Mantis led the way to the staircase and the three bugs started up it. The railing was rickety, and the plaster was crumbling from the wall, showing the laths beneath, like the ribs of a dusty skeleton.

"A pleasant ascent," said Pleasant Beetle. "Humble, yes, but not without a quaint charm."

The stairs were uneven, some of them rotten, a few missing entirely. Mantis pointed to the thin thread of glue that ran up them. He and his companions crested the staircase, into a hallway lit by the flame of a single lamp. The wall surrounding it was black with soot, and dustballs lay along the floor molding. The low sound of voices came from one of the rooms, and at that moment the door swung open and a tableful of vicious-looking ticks could be seen, playing cards. The door had been opened by one of them, who was in the process of pitching out a young doodlebug. "And don't come back until you have more money," said the tick, as the doodlebug bounced against the far wall and turned slowly around, a dazed look on his immature face.

"Come in, yer grace," said the tick, motioning to Pleasant Beetle. "A fresh hand is always welcome at our friendly little game."

"That's uncommonly pleasant of you," said Pleasant Beetle.

"They'll cheat you!" shouted the addled doodlebug. "And then throw you out."

"Surely not," said Pleasant Beetle.

"Right this way, m'lord," smiled the tick, and the ticks at the table smiled too, and waved to Pleasant Beetle.

"I say," said Pleasant Beetle to his companions, "that is a most pleasing display of good fellowship."

"It is a display of cunning, greed, and deceit," said Mantis.

The doodlebug staggered past them. "I'm cleaned out. A week's wages gone."

"Let it be a lesson to you then," said Mantis.

"I'll never change," said the doodlebug. "I'm rotten to the core." And he swayed down the hallway toward the stairs.

"Honest admissions like that are very exceedingly pleasant to encounter," said Pleasant Beetle. "A bug who can look at himself and speak the truth, however harsh, is to be commended. Pleasing behavior, yes, very pleasing."

"Come along," said Mantis, putting his hand to Pleasant Beetle's back. "We have work to do."

The tick said, "The door's open, gents, if you get the urge for a bit of sport."

Mantis slammed the door with one swipe of his long arm, then led the way to room 22. He tapped lightly. There was no answer. He pushed the door, and it swung open. They entered the darkened room, and Doctor Hopper found the gas lamp. The flame leapt up, lighting the room.

"Good heavens!"

Glued upside down to the wall was the glue worm, his arms outstretched, his legs moving feebly. He appeared disoriented.

"A blow to the head, I believe, Doctor," said Mantis.

"Yes," said Hopper, "it's raised a nasty bruise."

"Well, let's rotate him," said Mantis, and they did, with some difficulty, as he was covered with glue.

"Dratted stuff...what a mess..." Doctor Hopper's sleeve as well as the rim of his derby hat became stuck to the wall.

"Have a care...don't just peel me off..." muttered the glue worm. He was now upright, facing them, but was no better for it. His eyes had a dull look and his mouth hung open stupidly. Nonetheless, his protective coloring was functional, and his form blended into the dull, dirty gray of the wall to which he was attached.

"Pleasant Beetle," said Mantis, "I'm afraid we are not at the end of our chase."

"Eh? Why not? Isn't this the fellow who stole the Mealybug necklace?"

"Indeed. But I'd be much surprised if he had it any longer. He's obviously a blockhead."

The glue worm, on hearing this, laughed the laugh of a buffoon, and called for a cup of bee ale.

"He was hired for his sticky qualities," said Mantis. "Isn't that right, Mr. Glue Worm?"

"A blow to the head, I believe, Doctor"

"...stick with...Glue Worm..."

"A memorable motto, but not quite what we want to hear."

"...I'm stuck...on you..." sang the Glue Worm, badly out of tune, while gesturing stupidly with his six hands.

"A blockhead and a lout," said Mantis. "I doubt if he even remembers who hired him, banged him on the head, and then glued him to his own wall. Let us examine the room."

"...I'm glued to you...though and through..."

"A pleasant enough voice," said Pleasant Beetle. "Don't you think? Untrained, yes, but with a lilting sense of melody..."

The room was shabby, and held nothing but a rickety table and chair, and a sagging bed. Pleasant Beetle stroked each piece of furniture lightly with his cane. "Comfortable furnishings, which, by their simplicity, charm the heart. Here, one feels, a modest life is lived. I ask you, gentlemen, what could be more pleasant?"

Mantis seemed not to hear Pleasant Beetle's pleasantries, but was intently studying the area between the glue worm and the door. "Ah ha!"

"What is it, Mantis?" asked Doctor Hopper, hurrying to the detective's side.

"Two things, Doctor, to which I should like to draw your attention. Separately they would mean nothing, but taken together, they present us with a priceless clue." Mantis pointed to the edge of the rickety table. "What do you see here?"

"A drop of blood."

"Yes, and it is fresh. What does that suggest?"

"That some sort of bloodsucker has been here. Mosquito, perhaps."

"But look closely beside the speck of blood. What do you see?"

Doctor Hopper touched his fingertip to a tiny bit of yellow powder. "Why, it's pollen."

"Suggesting?"

"Butterfly or bee."

"So, Doctor, were there two guests here to see our Mr. Glue Worm? A bloodsucker and a bee?"

"It would appear so, yes."

"And yet you will notice the pollen and blood are in close proximity, and form a little trail to the door, in a pattern that is too regular to have been left by two guests. Blood and pollen overlap in the same way in each instance and point to their having been left by one guest and one guest only."

A frown had crossed Doctor Hopper's brow. "A bloodsucking pollen feeder?"

"Yes, Doctor. And you have seen him before."

"I? But where?"

"In Lettuce Land, during your army days."

Doctor Hopper thought for a moment, then struck his forehead with the flat of his hand. "By Jove, the Pangonia Lancer Flies! It comes back to me now, of course. They served with our regiment, and served bravely. The Pangonia flies were as fierce as the devil when it came to sucking blood from the enemy, yet after the battle they'd go off and uncurl their noses into a flower, for they loved pollen with a passion."

"Just so. And I'd say the Pangonia fly who visited this room had a taste for diamonds as well."

"Gad, sir," cried Pleasant Beetle, "your powers of deduction are supernatural!"

"Not at all. They are within the reach of anyone with a bit of patience."

"Your modesty becomes you, Inspector. I find that exceedingly pleasant."

"The question now," said Mantis, "is where do we look for this Pangonia fly?"

"Well," said Doctor Hopper, "I suggest we visit the Regimental Club."

"Right you are, Doctor." Mantis nodded toward the door. "There is nothing more for us here."

"And what about him?" Hopper indicated the glue worm. "He is, after all, a thief."

"He is soon to undergo metamorphosis, Doctor. Notice the bits of trash he has already glued to himself. It is with such trash that the glue worm weaves his cocoon. In a few days he'll be completely covered, and will slowly transform himself into a glue fly. We can only hope his new life will be an improvement on the old."

"You're a generous fellow, Mantis," said Pleasant Beetle, and turned toward the babbling glue worm. "For he is a wretched creature, and to be pitied."

"...just a little glue...keeps me stuck on you..."

"Reform yourself, sir," said Pleasant Beetle to the glue worm. "You could have a musical career. Not to the heights, perhaps, but on a street corner, where you could bring happiness to your fellow bug."

"Come along, Pleasant Beetle," said Mantis, with icy impatience.

"Sorry, old chap. Doing it again, I suppose? Much too pleasant, of course, but I do so like a pleasantry or two before parting."

"A lost moment here could cost us the necklace."

"Then let us be off, at once!"

Doctor hopper still retained his rank of captain in the Royal Army Medical Corps, and was an occasional visitor to the Regimental Club. He led Mantis and Pleasant Beetle to it now, to the ornate front doors, which were watched over by a pair of armed stag beetles, big fellows with glistening armor plate. They sprang to attention as Doctor Hopper and his guests came up the stairs. This outer formality gave way to an air of joviality inside. There were army ants, bombardier beetles, hawk moths, shield bugs, and many other military types. They were gathered around the billiard table and the piano, as well as at the nectar bar.

Doctor Hopper scanned the room for a familiar face, and found one seated in a large easy chair near the fireplace. "There's General Horse Stinger," said Hopper.

"Retired now, and a regular old gossip. He knows everyone in the regiment." Hopper led the way to General Horse Stinger's chair, and presented himself to the general, who rose at once.

"There's General Horse Stinger"

"Upon my word, it's Hopper! Sit down, sit down. Are these gentlemen with you?" The general snapped his fingers for a waiter. "Nectar for these chaps."

"General," said Hopper, "this is Cedric Pleasant Beetle. He's a close friend of Colonel Mealybug."

"Delighted to meet you, Pleasant Beetle, delighted. Any friend of Mealy's is welcome in my tent."

Pleasant Beetle was deeply pleased by this, and went into his usual display of pleasantries until General Horse Stinger cut him off. "Yes, yes, right you are. And this other gentleman?" He was now looking at Mantis.

"Inspector Mantis, at your service," said the detective with a slight bow of his long, lean body.

"I know you," said Horse Stinger. "Some years back. You—"

"—found the regimental silver when it was stolen. Yes," said Mantis, "I had the honor of rendering that slight service."

"The service was far from slight, sir. That silver was worth a fortune. Given to us by the Empress Moth of Bugland herself."

"Mantis," said Hopper, in surprise, "I knew nothing of this."

"You were in Lettuce Land at the time, Doctor." Mantis gave his thin smile, and seated himself beside General Horse Stinger. "General, we're hoping you might be of assistance to us."

"Anything at all. The Regiment does not forget those who have aided her in her time of need." Horse Stinger twisted the end of his thick mustache, which draped over each side of the fine stinger for which he was famed. "Fire away."

"A valuable necklace has been stolen. I'm sorry to say we suspect a member of the Pangonia Lancers."

"Fierce lads, the Pangonias. Fought their way out of some terrible jams. But they were peculiar. If they couldn't stick their face in a flower each day they got down in the dumps. That sort of temperament is liable to run to the bad if not carefully supervised." General Horse Stinger sipped his nectar thoughtfully. His medals, of which he had a chest full, sparkled in the light of the fireplace. "Do we think he's a Lancer down on his luck? Desperate, do anything for money? Something of a wastrel?"

"No, General. I think he is both clever and patient, with expensive tastes."

"Hmmmm." The General stared into the fire, his fingers in his mustache again, twisting it first one way, then the other. "Yes, there is a chap. Comes in here infrequently. Beautiful uniform, privately tailored, that sort of thing. Carries himself like a prince. Affected, certainly, but not someone to trifle with, as he is very good with a sword. What is his name, give me a half a tick." The General sat back in his chair, twisted his mustache again, then said, "Raif Pangofly! That's it! Captain Raif Pangofly. Swaggers in, buys nectar for everyone, gambles wildly, not caring if he wins or loses. Yes, that's the fellow you want."

"And where do we find Captain Pangofly?" asked Mantis.

"He has rooms near here on Silk Street. Ask around once you get there. A number of officers live on the block. Very posh neighborhood. Too expensive for an old pensioner like me."

"We are indebted to you, General."

"Remember, Mantis—swords, knives, he knows how to use them."

"I shall deal with him," said Mantis, softly, in a tone that sent a shiver of apprehension through Pleasant Beetle's antennas.

SILK STREET had many nightclubs and dance halls, and a great number of colorful revelers on the sidewalks—gaudy butterflies and beetles, as well as a rougher crowd—leather-jackets, water boatmen, wolf spiders, stone-flies, punkies, and screw worms. Pinching bugs were in the crowd, picking pockets. In the cafés, measuring-worms argued philosophy, and kissing bugs kissed as kissing bugs will. From the military caste there was a rowdy bunch of hickory horned devils flirting with some painted ladies from a nearby theatrical revue. "How very pleasant," said Pleasant Beetle to Mantis and Doctor Hopper as they walked through the crowd. "All these young people expressing themselves. I do so enjoy a bit of fun."

They stopped at a café and sat down at a table beside an elite group of soldiers—ambush bugs, clad in berets worn at a jaunty angle, and wearing bright braided lanyards through the epaulets of their uniforms.

"Stand them a round of the best nectar, Pleasant Beetle," said Mantis.

"It would give me great pleasure," said Pleasant Beetle. "Gentlemen—" He bowed toward the ambush bugs. "—won't you join me in a toast to her Highness, the Empress Moth of Bugland?"

The drinks were brought and the ambush bugs drank the toast, and called Pleasant Beetle a good fellow. "Thank you, gentlemen, thank you. It's most pleasant of you to say so, and may I return the compliment by saying I have never seen such pleasing uniforms as those you wear. So brightly colored, so impeccably designed. You are the pride of Bugland, sirs. Our country is safe in your hands."

The ambush bugs called him a splendid fellow, several more rounds were purchased for them, and soon the two tables were exchanging easy conversation.

"I wonder if you might help us," said Doctor Hopper. "We're looking for an old comrade of ours. I served with him in Lettuce Land. He's a member of the Pangonia Lancers. Chap named Raif Pangofly."

"I know him," said a lieutenant of the Ambushers. "You'll find him at the Moon Moth Club. He's there every night these days."

"—won't you join me in a toast to her Highness"

THE MOON MOTH CLUB was a romantic place, its entrance painted with two huge eyes like those on the wings of a moth.

Doctor Hopper led the way into an enchanting atmosphere. The ceiling was hung in plush folds of red velvet, so the club seemed to be inside the petals of a rose. Fireflies waited on tables, their abdomens glowing in the darkened room. On stage a slender fruitworm sang to the music of a grasshopper band.

Pleasant Beetle slipped the headwaiter a very large bribe and he and Mantis and Hopper were shown to a table that commanded a view of the entire club. The fruitworm finished his song and a pair of wrigglers in abbreviated costume came out, performing an exotic dance.

"Remarkable," observed Pleasant Beetle, as he watched the wrigglers. "Never seen anything quite like it, Hopper, have you?"

"No, Pleasant Beetle, I haven't."

"One wonders how they can be so... so flexible."

"There's Captain Raif Pangofly," said Mantis, coldly.

Seated a few tables away was a ferocious looking officer of the Pangonia Lancers. As General Horse Stinger had said, his uniform was perfectly tailored. His trousers were black with a wide red stripe up the seam. An immaculate red silk cape hung from his shoulders and a sash of red silk crossed his chest. His hat, which lay on the table, had a brilliant red plume affixed to it. Seated beside him was a moon moth of statuesque beauty, over whom the fireflies fussed.

"Notice their interaction with her," said Mantis. "In the few minutes we've been here, they have already consulted with her on several matters of management. She is the moon moth for whom the club is named." Mantis had rested his elbows on the table, and his long fingers were folded together. "And she is about to receive a present from her dashing Captain Pangofly."

"The necklace? Has Pangofly got it with him?" asked Pleasant Beetle.

"Yes. And he has the look of a rogue who has met his match," said Mantis.

"Eh?"

The Moon Moth Club was a romantic place

"We know from the method of the robbery that Captain Pangofly is coolly calculating, but observe: he has already put his hand to an inner pocket nervously, not once but twice, yet come out with nothing. He hesitates to present the necklace because he is in awe of her."

"She is a stunner," said Doctor Hopper.

Mantis lifted an eyebrow coolly toward Hopper, who harummphed several times, then said, "Well, dash it all, Mantis, she is a stunner. Even an iceberg like you can see that."

"I see that Pangofly's a fool, and that she has bewitched him."

Doctor Hopper had to agree to that. The moon moth was obviously toying with the infatuated Lancer, fanning her beautiful wings at him, then covering her face behind them, so that only her dark eyes were visible. Her antennas, which she had adorned with tiny jewels, swayed back and forth before Captain Pangofly's eyes and the besotted warrior swayed with them.

"What a magnificent creature," said Doctor Hopper. "What does she see in this Pangofly? He's obviously a bounder."

"I'd say she sees a man who wouldn't hesitate to steal for her," said Mantis, dryly.

"You insist on casting her in a poor light, Mantis. But how do you know the secrets of her soul?"

"I know," said Mantis, even more dryly.

"There!" exclaimed Pleasant Beetle. "He is giving her the necklace!"

The debonair Lancer was holding the necklace out toward the moon moth. At a nod from her he rose and hung it around her slender neck. It sparkled softly, picking up the light of the fireflies who gathered to admire it.

"He's a brazen fellow," said Hopper. "Giving it to her in public."

"The best place to hide something everyone is looking for is under their noses," observed Mantis.

"So now what do we do?" asked Pleasant Beetle.

"Doctor Hopper is going to go over and insult Captain Pangofly."

"Steady on, Mantis," said Hopper. "Insulting chaps isn't my line."

"He is giving her the necklace!"

"While you are creating this diversion, I will put myself in position."

"Why don't you insult him, and I'll put myself in position?" But Hopper knew it was pointless to argue with Mantis. The inspector had used him as decoy on several other occasions. And, reflected the good doctor, once it nearly cost me my life. Fascinating case, of course—poor Miss Juliana Butterfly, a circus performer, held in the clutches of the Tarantula. During the rescue the foul creature pumped his poison into me. A close shave, that. But we saved Miss Juliana Butterfly, and she was most grateful.

Hopper clutched his cane in his hand, tapped it several times in his palm, and then strode slowly toward the Lancer's table. As he did so, he caught sight of the gleaming dagger hanging from Captain Pangofly's belt. And, braced against the side of the captain's chair, was his sword. What if I grabbed it, wondered Hopper? And pointed it at him while calling him a blackguard?

He'd disarm me and then stab me through the heart. Not a pretty picture.

Verbal abuse, that's the ticket. Give him a good tongue lashing. And then hop out of harm's way. A good hop might carry me all the way to the door. Two hops and I'll be in the street.

A sound plan, with much to recommend it, especially the hopping.

And so, Doctor Hopper strode up to Captain Pangofly's table and pointing his cane at him contemptuously, said, "You, sir, are a cad."

"And you, sir, are a dead man." Pangofly calmly turned toward the moon moth. "Would you excuse me a moment, my dear? I must deal with this impudent idiot."

The moon moth gazed at Hopper, her eyes showing curiosity and something like amusement. Hopper had no time to consider the import of this, for Captain Pangofly was getting out of his chair. "How do you wish to die, little idiot? By sword or dagger?"

"Before we go into that, Pangofly, you might explain how you come to be in the possession of a valuable necklace belonging to Colonel Mealybug."

Pangofly's eyebrow arched just slightly. "To your idiocy you add slander." He reached for his sword. "What a pity I can only kill you once."

Hopper put a hand in his pocket. "I warn you, I'm armed." His fingers closed on a piece of chocolate.

"Armed? What audacity." The lancer's hand closed around the hilt of his sword. But the fingers of the moon moth fell upon his wrist. "Ignore him, Raif. I'll have him removed from the club."

"My dear, I mean to remove him from existence altogether."

"You'll not take me so easily," said Hopper, and braced himself for some vigorous hopping.

"He's a charming little fellow," said the moon moth. "And so brave."

Hopper forgot all thought of hopping, removed his derby hat and placed it over his heart, as he bowed to her. "Doctor Howard Hopper, Madame. I realize you are innocent of any wrongdoing. You have been misled by this criminal."

Pangofly calmly drew his sword. "You shall die now."

"I don't think so," said a soft voice from behind him, and before

Pangofly could turn, the long arm of Inspector Mantis closed around his neck. The captain threw his sword down and reached for his dagger but Mantis's other arm pinned his before he could free the blade from its scabbard.

"I'll destroy you," hissed Pangofly.

"Confident fellow," mused Mantis, as he tightened his hold. In all of Bugland, there was no insect with a stronger grip. The captain tried to hurl himself forward, but it was as if bars of iron held him in place. He couldn't move his head. He couldn't lift his arms. And he could barely breathe.

"Curse...you...whoever you are..."

"I am no one at all," said Mantis, his voice undisturbed by his strenuous effort.

"I'll...be...revenged..." gasped Pangofly. The room was spinning. The captain's eyes swelled out, his veins bulged, and then his body went limp.

Mantis released him and Pangofly fell to the floor, unconscious.

"Forgive me, Madame," said Mantis, turning to the moon moth. "I must now collect the necklace you're wearing, for it is stolen and I have been hired to see that it is returned to its owner."

The moon moth smiled as she unclasped the necklace. "I have no need of it." She extended her graceful arm toward him, the necklace dangling between her fingers. "Take it." The necklace dropped into Mantis's hand. "I didn't know it was stolen."

"Of course," said Mantis, with what Doctor Hopper thought was unnecessary cynicism.

"We know you are completely blameless in this matter," said Hopper, quickly. "How could you have known the necklace was stolen? You are not made for coarse matters. Yours is the realm of beauty and sweetness. May I offer you—" He brought his hand out of his pocket. "—a piece of chocolate?"

The butterfly smiled. "Then this is what you were armed with? Chocolate? Against the greatest swordsman in Bugland? You are

The long arm of Inspector Mantis closed around his neck.

brave." She took the piece of offered chocolate. "I shall treasure it more than any necklace." She let her fingertip trail over Doctor Hopper's palm. "Because it came from you."

Hopper felt giddy from his head to his toes. Indeed, he felt near to swooning. A confirmed bachelor, his palm was seldom, if ever, stroked. And the moon moth was the loveliest creature he'd ever seen. "I am...honored, Madame."

"We shall be friends," said the moon moth.

"I'm not worthy of such friendship," said Hopper, and so nervous was he now, he chewed the brim of his derby hat.

The moon moth squeezed his hand in hers as she opened her dazzling wings. "Scandal would be ruinous to the Moon Moth Club. I hope your companions—" She cast a sideways glance toward Mantis and Pleasant Beetle. "—aren't going to cause trouble."

"There's no danger of that. I have considerable influence with these gentlemen." Hopper drew himself up to his full height between Mantis and Pleasant Beetle.

The moon moth fanned her wings toward him, their luminous edges lightly caressing his cheek. "You'll be a guest here often, I'm sure. When you come ask for me. And I shall join you, at a table just for two." She slipped from her chair, stepped over the unconscious Pangofly, and glided away with her fireflies in attendance.

"Gad, what a creature," sighed Hopper.

"And for all we know she is innocent," said Mantis. "Though I very much doubt it. But it's no business of ours, now that you have pledged your word to her."

"I did so happily," said Hopper.

"We can see that," smiled Mantis, not unpleasantly. The necklace had been found, which was his only concern. He looked down at Captain Pangofly. "I seem to have throttled him within an inch of his life."

Doctor Hopper bent and touched the fallen lancer's wrist. "His pulse is strong. He'll be coming around any moment."

—

Mantis removed a flower from a vase on the table and placed it on Pangofly's chest, directly beneath his curled-up proboscis. "That should improve his disposition."

Pangofly gave a groan and opened his eyes. His proboscis unrolled and went straight into the flower's heart, from which he sucked its nectar dry. Then his eyes met Mantis's. "You attacked me from behind."

"An army must guard its back as well as its front, Captain," said Mantis.

"True enough." Pangofly brought himself to a sitting position and rubbed his neck. "You have the grip of a fiend."

"You have served Bugland bravely, Captain. My friends and I, therefore, shall keep silent about this matter of the necklace. The only other person who knows of it is General Horse Stinger and he will close ranks with you, I feel certain."

Pangofly rose to his feet and straightened his swordbelt. "I ask you again, sir—who are you?"

"And I tell you again—I am no one."

"Very well," said Pangofly. "I will not pry." He retrieved his fallen sword and put it in its scabbard. "I've brought disgrace on myself with this affair." He nodded toward the moon moth, who was now at the far end of the club, speaking to other guests. "Bewitching, isn't she?"

"I am indifferent to her, I'm afraid," said Mantis.

"Lucky chap." Pangofly picked up his dagger and sheathed it. "You have spared my reputation. I will be rejoining my regiment in Lettuce Land, for the far hills are the only place for a blackguard such as I. But should you need my hand in any matter, contact the Pangonia Lancers, and I shall find my way to you."

"Thank you, Captain. I hope I shall have no need of your aid."

"One never knows when one might be outnumbered. Therefore I take this oath on my sword—" He slapped its hilt. "—I am your ally in whatever befalls you."

Then Captain Pangofly turned slowly in the direction of the moon moth, who did not so much as glance his way. "Farewell, my love," he said in a rough whisper, and did an abrupt about-face. Swirling his cape around him, he crossed the floor of the club and departed.

"Well," said Mantis, "I think our business here is completed."

"Colonel Mealybug will be delighted when I give him back the necklace," said Pleasant Beetle. "It will be such a pleasant moment. I'm quite looking forward to it."

Pleasant Beetle and Mantis started across the floor of the club with Doctor Hopper following them. Hopper's eyes were on the moon moth, whose white wings were now wrapped around her in a luminous sheathe. Her statuesque figure towered over the crowd, and over him as he passed by. He was already feeling quite silly about giving her his candy, and absolving her of all guilt, and chewing his hat brim. You're a fool, Hopper, he said to himself. Now leave, without another word to her.

And then the lacy edge of her wing floated out and touched the back of his neck. "Good-bye, my friend," she said in a whisper. "You won't forget me, will you?"

"Never!" cried Hopper, and rushed from the club.

{ ☀ }

"Never!" cried Hopper, and rushed from the club.

THE CASE OF THE INVISIBLE HAND

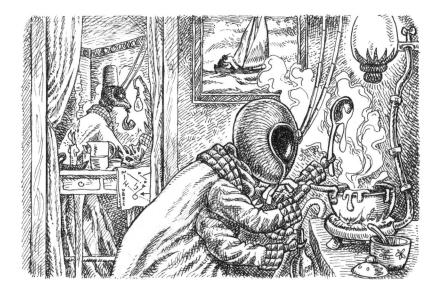

DOCTOR HOPPER was at the little gas ring fire, preparing a batch of jellybeans. He stirred the mixture with concentration, checking the temperature constantly. "Anything hotter than 230 degrees and they'll come out too hard," he cautioned himself. "And a hard jellybean is unacceptable."

He heard Mantis muttering to himself in the next room where the inspector's makeshift chemical laboratory was set up, much to the dislike of their landlady, Mrs. Inchworm.

"She has a point, of course," said Hopper to himself. "Mantis's chemical concoctions produce a terrible smell on occasion, which can be devilishly hard to get rid of. While the jellybean—" He stirred in some grape flavoring. "—the jellybean is an entirely wholesome, sweet-smelling—"

A tremendous explosion issued from the next room, blowing Mantis clear through the door, across the floor and into a heap in the corner. His smoking jacket was on fire and his fez was burnt to a crisp but he had a triumphant smile on his face.

"I've done it, Hopper."

"I should say you have, old man. I hear Mrs. Inchworm on the stairs."

The landlady burst in. "Heaven help us!" she cried. "The wallpaper is ablaze."

"I have isolated and then combined the chemical components used by the bombardier beetle."

"Get some water!" shouted Mrs. Inchworm.

"They are hydroquinone and hydrogen peroxide. The beetle carries them in reservoirs in his rear, if I may put it graphically."

"Put it out!" cried Mrs. Inchworm, pointing at the wallpaper, on which little tongues of flame were dancing.

Hopper beat at the flames with his hat while Mantis picked up a teapot and emptied it on his smoking jacket, which was indeed smoking.

"The wallpaper, Mr. Mantis, if you would please," snapped Mrs. Inchworm.

"Ah, yes, I see." Mantis found the pitcher they used for washing up after tea. He threw its contents at the wallpaper, extinguishing the flames. "Now, as I was saying, the bombardier beetle—"

"Bother the beetle," said Mrs. Inchworm, stamping out burning embers on the rug.

"He would be a bother, Mrs. Inchworm, if you were to be caught in a blast from his nether region. The gas he emits is extremely hot, as this wallpaper and my smoking jacket show."

"I don't go around stirring up beetles," said Mrs. Inchworm.

"And very wise you are in that respect," said Mantis. "The bug who does stir one up will hear a loud popping sound and wish he hadn't. The sound, of course, is the opening of the valve in the bombardier's backside from which the mixture flows. I seem to have destroyed my hat." He looked at its sooty remains.

"This wallpaper must come down," said Mrs. Inchworm, sadly.

"The wallpaper is fine, Mrs. Inchworm," said Mantis. "I'm indifferent to these domestic touches."

"Well, I'm not," said Mrs. Inchworm. "I'll order some new wallpaper and give you the bill."

"As you wish," said Mantis. "Doctor Hopper and I will pay it happily."

"Speak for yourself, Mantis," said Hopper. "Furthermore, these jellybeans are hard as a rock. And do you know why?"

"The preparation of jellybeans is not one of my interests," said Mantis.

"They were overheated. From your ridiculous explosion."

"Untimely perhaps. But not ridiculous. The information gathered here today may prove invaluable at a later date."

They were interrupted by a faint scratching at the door.

"It's probably that dogfly from next door," said Mrs. Inchworm, crossly. "It always comes around when you're cooking something sweet."

"Mrs. Inchworm, the cooking of sweets is a harmless hobby of mine," said Doctor Hopper. "And I'm not about to give it up because of a dogfly."

Mrs. Inchworm opened the door. It was not the dogfly. It was a prostrate ant, her feeble feelers working the air.

Doctor Hopper crouched over the fallen ant. "Mrs. Inchworm, my jellybean mixture, quickly."

Mrs. Inchworm brought the pan and Hopper broke off the few undamaged pieces and gave them to the ant. She swallowed desperately and asked for more. The rich mixture brought about an immediate revival. She sat up, shook her feelers, and smiled.

"I think," said Hopper, looking at Mrs. Inchworm, "the value of the jellybean has been vividly demonstrated."

"Well, she looks a great deal better, I'll say that."

The ant swayed back and forth, regaining her balance slowly. Finally she said, with a distinct accent of the North Bugland farm country, "That was a fine snack. I'm obliged to your worship."

"And your name, miss?" asked Mrs. Inchworm.

"Adora, ma'am." The ant blushed, as if to say she could not live up to her name. Then regaining her momentum, she declared, "I've come on important business."

"Please," said Hopper, "take a seat. You're not completely recovered."

Adora took a seat and arranged her legs primly as she continued looking around, confusion in her expression. "Where are the offices?"

"Offices?"

"Isn't this the Farm Management Bureau?"

"The Farm Management Bureau is down the street," said Inspector Mantis, coming toward her. "You have come by accident to the home of Mrs. Inchworm." He nodded toward his landlady respectfully, for he knew he must tread carefully, having ignited her wallpaper. "But it is also where I receive clients and I'd say you should become one immediately."

"And who might you be, sir, when you're not on fire?" She was looking at his burnt hat and singed smoking jacket.

Inspector Mantis drew nearer to her. "You are you an aphid herder?"

Adora looked at him in astonishment. "How did you know?"

"All aphid herders smell of nectar. A charming scent which you have been emitting since you fell on our doorstep." He brushed burnt fabric from the cuff of his smoking jacket, then reached out and plucked a transparent bit of something from Adora's feeler. He held it up to the light. "A portion of an aphid wing. The vein pattern is quite distinctive." He tossed the wing on the floor, his interest in it over.

Adora was looking at Mantis as if he were a wizard. Mantis said to her, "Such deductions are nothing. A much greater mystery surrounds you. Tell me why you came to the city."

"It's a terrible thing. Supernatural is what it is."

"I very much doubt that."

"Well," said Adora, smoothing out her rough herder's skirt, "the food is being taken from my mouth by a spirit I call the Invisible Hand." She peered at Mantis defiantly. "If that ain't supernatural, I don't know what is."

"Tell me more about this Invisible Hand," said Mantis, lighting his

"And who might you be, sir, when you're not on fire?"

pipe. He began to throw his match on the floor, met Mrs. Inchworm's eye, and placed it carefully in an ashtray.

"How can I tell you about the Invisible Hand? I've never seen it."

"But it takes the food from your mouth?"

"It's why I arrived here near dead. I haven't eaten in weeks."

"Continue," said Mantis, puffing on his pipe.

"I milk one of my aphids but no sooner is the nectar in my mouth than it's gone again. Taken by the Invisible Hand."

"Are you fully conscious during this remarkable feat?"

"Of course I am! But the Invisible Hand is fast." She looked at Hopper. "Begging your pardon, sir, but do you have any more of that delicious snack you gave me? I'm still feeling just a bit weak."

"Owing to an explosion—" Hopper looked at Mantis. "—what remains of the mixture is now inedible. But fudge is always available." He went to his fudge cabinet and took out a sizable piece. "There you are, miss. Like the jellybean, fudge has powerful restorative qualities. I recommend it to all my patients."

"You're a doctor?"

"Doctor Hopper, at your service." He gave her a little bow, then pointed to Mantis. "And this gentleman is Inspector Mantis, the greatest consulting detective in the world. You can rely on us to help you solve this business of the Invisible Hand."

"Do you charge?" she asked, uneasily, for the farmers of North Bugland are known to be close with their money.

Hopper said, "A cup of your splendid aphid nectar will be payment enough." He looked at Mantis. "Eh, Mantis?"

Mantis waved his pipe indifferently. Money meant nothing to him when crime was afoot. He said to the distraught ant, "You can add nothing to this account of yours regarding the Invisible Hand?"

"Nothing," said Adora.

Mantis looked toward Hopper. "I think, Doctor, it is time we paid a call on Boring Beetle."

"Must we, Mantis?"

"His knowledge of arcane matters is without equal."

"Very well," said Hopper, resigning himself to an excruciating encounter with the great scholar and explorer.

WHEN THEY REACHED THE LECTURE HALL, students were staggering into the street, their eyelids drooping.

"I see Boring Beetle has not lost his touch," said Mantis.

He led the way into the hall. Progress wasn't easy, as students had rolled into the aisles, overcome by sleep. Those who remained in their seats were nodding off, yawning, or staring numbly toward the lectern.

Boring Beetle was at the lectern. "Our expedition was under the leadership of Sir Malcolm Mealybug, courageous but stooped in stature as were other members of his illustrious family, one of whom had no mouth, which was of course unfortunate, yet it contributed to the family motto Never Daunted which you will find in my compendium, Mottos of Old Bugland, which summarizes a larger work, Battle Banners of Bugland, a title I hope you will bear in mind…"

Unable to bear it in mind, a student in front of Mantis fell out of his seat into the aisle, snoring loudly.

Boring Beetle continued: "Sir Malcolm entered the Lost City of the Termites, and we followed him. Desiccated heads lay everywhere. He shone his lantern on an ancient fungus garden in ruin. His motto, Never Daunted, served him well now for the air was filled with the nasty smell of a foul-smelling sticky liquid which stuck to my shoe, shoes which I purchased in a little shop in Shade Tree many years ago from a cobbler who built the shoe around my foot as I stood there watching the passing panorama of traders from every part of the world, one of whom I shall always remember for he left a remarkable trail of slime behind him, not, I should say, a particularly appealing advertisement for what he sold, though he beat a drum of a kind I'd not seen before, made from the abdomen of a grub, primitive yes, but with a resounding little tone which, if I heard it today would carry me back to Shade Tree, carry me on the wings of song…"

Unconscious bugs were being carried on the wings of friends, up the aisles and out of the lecture hall. Hopper, Mantis, and Adora took empty seats in the first row. Boring Beetle plunged on.

"The foul-smelling substance in the Lost City was of course sprayed by termite soldiers on their invaders; that it still stuck to my shoe after hundreds of years is proof of what we bugs are capable of producing, if we put our minds to it." Boring Beetle rapped his fist for emphasis on the lectern, startling a few sleepers back to consciousness. "My shoe remains in a peculiar condition."

They immediately fell back to sleep.

"The foul smell has remained on that shoe no matter what I treat it with. With such a powerful defense mechanism, you are surely wondering how the soldiers of the Lost City lost the battle."

No one was wondering. Everyone in the auditorium, with one exception, had gone to sleep. Hopper snored in his hat. Adora's head was between her knees. Only Mantis remained awake, but his eyes were closing and he just managed to say, "Boring Beetle, I must consult with you."

Boring Beetle stopped, peered down toward the first row. "Mantis, is it you?"

"It is, and the matter is urgent."

"I daresay it is, but I must think of my students."

"They're unconscious, Boring Beetle."

Boring Beetle peered around the lecture hall. "So they are." Boring Beetle closed his notes and descended from the lectern.

Hopper came awake with a jolt. "Ah, Boring Beetle, a most interesting point you were making. Put very well."

"Thank you, Doctor. A shoe that can't be cleaned, a smell that never goes away, surely it forces us to further inquiry which—"

Hopper's head went down to his chest again, the tone of Boring Beetle's voice like a switch that sent one immediately to sleep.

Mantis, struggling to remain conscious, gripped Boring Beetle's arm. "What do you know of parasitic attacks?"

"They're unconscious, Boring Beetle."

"Everything."

"Good. Come with us."

Mantis woke Doctor Hopper again, then Adora Ant. They left the lecture hall with Boring Beetle. Students were asleep on the lecture hall stairs, others were recovering on the grass. "Conscientious students, Mantis, who study long into the night. Thus you see them, catching a few winks while they can." He peered at Adora. "I don't believe I've met this young lady."

"This is Adora Ant, a client of Mantis," said Hopper.

"Charmed, dear lady," said Boring Beetle, bowing over her outstretched hand.

"Howdy do," said Adora.

"Your accent is North Bugland, province of Egg, if I'm not mistaken."

"Indeed it is, sir. And a nicer place you'd never want to live in until the Invisible Hand come around."

Here Mantis explained the situation of Adora Ant, as Boring Beetle listened, nodding his head and sweeping his antennas back and forth over her as if making some subtle determination regarding her. "I see, I see. Parasitic activity, Mantis, just as you say. A significant work was written on the subject some years ago only to be destroyed by a paper-eating parasite." Again his antennas swept the air, curling and uncurling. "It was a boring work, if I may say so."

"You would certainly know."

"And no great loss because, as I say, I know everything on the subject." He turned to Adora. "When the Invisible Hand struck did you hear any sound?"

"I can't say that I did."

"A very thin high-pitched sound? Think…"

"I don't know," said Adora, nervously. "I was busy trying to eat."

Boring Beetle spoke, as if to himself. "Yes, the sound is cleverly blended into the ambient noise and so goes unnoticed."

Mantis gripped his arm firmly. "What are you suggesting, Boring Beetle?"

"You asked me if I knew about parasitic attacks. Well, this is one of the more diabolical ones. The method is known. It was described by Professor Beanweevil in a delightful little work—"

"The point, Boring Beetle."

"Hypnotic sound, Mantis. Stupefies the victim. Or renders her unconscious, as I believe happened to this poor creature." Boring Beetle pressed the hand of Adora Ant protectively.

"Thank you, sir, I'm sure. But I don't remember no sound."

"Perfectly all right, my dear. It's a trifling thing." He turned back to Mantis. "As I say, the method is known. What isn't known is the bug who uses that method."

"How can that be, Boring Beetle?" asked Doctor Hopper. "Surely someone must have seen this villain sometime."

"Camouflage, Doctor Hopper, and mimicry. I refer you to my paper, Bugland Unknown. In it there is evidence that several million bugs live amongst us in complete disguise. Forever anonymous, forever a frustration for those who like to see things neatly ordered, numbered, and classified. I count myself among them and I daresay you, as a medical practitioner, feel the same."

Hopper's feelings on the matter were not aired. His eyelids had grown suddenly heavy and he was seeing jellybeans in his head, bright and bouncing. Good grief, I'm dreaming. He shook himself awake. "Sorry, Boring Beetle, you were saying?"

"Just this, Doctor. There is more in Bugland than any of us can ever know for the simple reason that we bugs are deeply mysterious beings."

To this, Mantis could only nod his head in agreement. He solved what mysteries he could, but all around them at every moment sinister activity was at work, cloaked and guarded.

"Well then," inquired Hopper of Boring Beetle, "how are we to catch this miscreant?"

"Chap I know, follow me." Boring Beetle led them away from the lecture hall, across the quadrangle of Bugland University, and into the common streets of the city. Hopper regretted the lack of jellybeans on the outing; had Mantis not exploded the mixture they could all be having a tasty treat. He searched his pockets, came up with an emergency square of fudge and gallantly offered it to Adora.

"Thank you, sir. Most generous of you, I'm sure. But I couldn't take your last bit of fudge."

"Nonsense," said Hopper. "You were robbed of your last good meal. You must keep up your strength."

Adora accepted the fudge gratefully. As she popped it past her lips, she looked around in anticipation of it being stolen right out of her mouth. "Have no fear," said Hopper, brandishing his cane. "I'll thrash any devil who tries to interfere with you."

Nonetheless Adora ate her fudge quickly while Boring Beetle swept his antennas across her head.

"What are you searching for, sir, if you don't mind my asking?"

"Secrets of the air, my dear," but Boring Beetle did not say more. And Hopper thought that Boring Beetle was himself something of a mystery —explorer, scholar, bore.

The streets were crowded now for they were approaching the theater district, a neighborhood Doctor Hopper knew well. For here he enjoyed performances by such notable music hall singers

The streets were crowded now for they were approaching the theater district.

as Dolly Damselfly, Vanessa Velvet-Ant, and of course the great
Maria Flowerfly. "By George, that reminds me—" He opened the
little medical bag he always carried with him. He'd entirely forgotten the medicinal cough drops tucked away there. Made by himself, cherry flavored to his exacting standards for the throat of Maria
Flowerfly. "Cough drop? Boring Beetle?"

"Thank you, Doctor." Boring Beetle popped the little offering into
his mouth. "Delicious."

Mantis ignored Hopper's outstretched hand. When on a case food
meant nothing to him. So Hopper and Adora finished the remaining cough drops. "I do love a sweet," admitted Adora. Her aphids
produced the sweetest nectar. Would she ever enjoy it again?

"You will, Adora Ant," said Mantis.

Shocked, she gazed at him, her mouth open. "You read minds?"

Mantis let the question hang. Her thought process had been so
obvious it wasn't worth mentioning. From sweets to her aphids and
their nectar was a predictable progression.

"You're a wizard," said Adora Ant. "That's what we need for this job."

Mantis could not be bothered to comment on this either. He was
not a wizard, nor was what he did a job. It was the fine art of detection.

But tonight Boring Beetle had the scent. And he must lead and
we follow humbly.

They were now in the heart of the theater district. It had its share of street entertainers. Some tumblebugs were performing backflips for the crowd, their nimble bodies floating through the air, legs waving.

There was also a bug who billed himself as the Amazing Cling Beetle. Ten strong bugs from the crowd pulled at him but could not detach him from a wall to which he clung with all six feet.

Police Officer Shield Bug came along, swinging his night stick nimbly. "All right, break it up there, before you pull the wall down." In fact, cracks were starting to appear. The beetle let go suddenly and everyone pulling at him fell on the pavement.

The Amazing Cling Beetle bowed grandly and then addressed the crowd. "A feat of strength such as you will not see every day or any day. A supernatural grip, my friends, you saw it with your own eyes."

"Sixty thousand glue-tipped bristles on his feet," said Boring Beetle softly to Adora Ant. "A perfectly natural secretion."

A few appreciative members of the crowd stuck coins on the Amazing Cling Beetle's bristles. Some drunken Army worms flipped candy wrappers and cigarette butts which also stuck.

"Move along there," said Officer Shield Bug to the Army worms. Then turning his head he said, "Inspector Mantis, I think?"

"At your service," said Mantis.

"Bugland Yard could use you, sir. Always unsolved cases going there."

"They have only to ask," said Mantis.

"They're too proud, sir, too proud. Well, excuse me, I've got to run off that bug up ahead. Making a dreadful racket."

The bug he referred to was a one-bug band, surrounded with battered instruments, some attached to his ankles, others to his wrists, bells dancing on his forehead as his foot kept time with a drum. In his arms string instruments coiled like snakes. Attached to his mouth was a pipe which made an assortment of sounds, imitating cicadas, crickets, grasshoppers —sounds to frighten enemies, to attract friends, to proclaim love. His repertoire seemed vast and he ran through it vigorously if deafeningly.

"That's enough of that," said Officer Shield Bug.

"A moment, please, officer," said Boring Beetle. "This fellow may be useful to us."

"And who might you be, sir?"

"Professor Boring Beetle, of Bugland University where I'm currently lecturing on the Lost City of the Termites, a place you'd probably find fascinating as it's filled with skulls, swords, and a mysterious substance that ruined my shoes, which should also be of some interest to you, for unless I miss my guess every police officer walking his beat knows the value of a fine pair of shoes."

Officer Shield Bug was swaying where he stood, struggling to stay awake. Boring Beetle's boring voice had cut through the noise of the street musician, striking Officer Shield Bug squarely between the antennas. Again Doctor Hopper noted, from a purely medical perspective, the numbing delivery of Boring Beetle. Several people in the crowd had fallen into the gutter and only by a tremendous effort of the will did Officer Shield Bug maintain consciousness. He waved his night stick and muttered, "Carry on," after which he went and stuck his head in a fountain.

"Boring Beetle," said Mantis, "your help is invaluable."

"Tut tut, my dear fellow, nothing to it."

Owing to the retreat of the police officer, the street musician had continued happily with his racket, imitating dozens if not hundreds of bugs. He was a swarm of songs, a torrent of tunes, strumming, ringing, chiming, chanting. He did the melody of the moth, the drone of the stable fly, the hymn of the honey bee. And suddenly Adora Ant froze, opened her mouth, and remained that way, catatonic.

"As I thought," said Boring Beetle. "Somewhere in all the noise this fellow is making is the Song of the Invisible Hand." He waved his great antennas like the conductor of a symphony, bringing the concert to a sudden halt.

The street musician stared at him. "Mr. Boring Beetle?"

Adora Ant had come back to consciousness the moment the

"That's enough of that," said Officer Shield Bug.

musician stopped playing. She looked at the group of bugs surrounding her. "What happened to me?"

"You were hypnotized," said Boring Beetle. "By this fellow. Allow me to introduce Ben Breeze Fly."

She looked at the ragged street performer. He seemed capable of nothing but a lot of noise, while she was a disciplined worker, herding her aphids from dawn until dusk. How could he have hypnotized her?

He said, "Light as a breeze, miss." He struck a pair of cymbals together, their tone high-pitched and pure. "On the breeze you hear Ben Breeze Fly's song."

Boring Beetle took a gold coin from his pocket, on which the portrait of Her Highness the Empress Moth was stamped, and said to Breeze Fly, "This is yours. But you must run through your entire repertoire."

"Are you sure, guv? We'll be here until tomorrow morning."

"It will be sufficient if you play a few bars of every song. That will tell us what we want to know."

"It won't have the beauty," protested Breeze Fly. "I always like a nice segue from tune to tune."

"An artist," said Boring Beetle, turning to Mantis. "One must, of course, respect the fine feeling he displays. While trekking in Pandorus, I camped in a little village. They fed me nectar and some delicious leaf I never properly identified or digested though it stained my lips as yellow as your socks. Meanwhile their local musician strummed on a one-stringed instrument that nearly drove me mad. I asked the chief to make him stop. Turns out it was the chief's son. A grave insult to the tribe. I barely escaped being boiled alive."

Breeze Fly fell into his instruments, eyes closed, feet in the air, bored into unconsciousness.

Doctor Hopper brought him around with smelling salts from his medical bag. "That's better."

Mantis said, "Let me handle this, Boring Beetle."

"Certainly, certainly." Boring Beetle stepped aside and Mantis gave Breeze Fly the downbeat.

The songs, or pieces of them, rolled out. During a particularly high-pitched whining air, Adora Ant's mouth fell open and her body stiffened.

"Stop!" ordered Mantis.

Breeze Fly frowned. "I was just getting warmed up."

"And repeat that last bit."

Adora Ant remained catatonic during the repetition of the sound.

"And there we have it," said Boring Beetle. "Where did you get that song, Ben?"

"Oh, I dunno. Just picked it up somewhere."

A second gold coin came from Boring Beetle's pocket. "Your Empress, Ben. To keep you company." He withdrew the coin as Breeze Fly reached for it. "First you must search your memory for the origin of the song."

"Well, let me see…" Breeze Fly began beating the drum with his foot as if he were tramping somewhere, instruments strapped to his back. "Yes, I remember. It was in Mine Town."

"That's near my aphid ranch," said Adora.

"A rough place," said Boring Beetle to Mantis, "awash with cheap nectar."

"They love me there," said Breeze Fly.

"There is room for doubt concerning that assertion but we'll let it pass," said Mantis. "Exactly where in Mine Town were you when you heard the sound?"

"Strolling up and down Main Street."

"And the sound?"

"Floated on the air. It could have come from anywhere. I tell you, they love me there."

Boring Beetle took Mantis aside. "We've learned all we can from this fellow."

The Bugland Follies let out, the crowd filling the sidewalk. Soon Doctor Hopper was surrounded by gorgeous bugs, their brilliant wings fanning the air. They were all patients of his, young ladies who enjoyed his sweet prescriptions. "Oh, Doctor," said Polly Pepper Moth, fluttering up to him, "I feel much more pep since taking that potion of yours." And she wrapped him enthusiastically inside her wings.

"I'm delighted," said Hopper, struggling to get free. He visited a great many charming females on his rounds, but this was embarrassing. His embarrassment increased as Consuela, a Spanish moon moth, shoved Polly aside. "Doc-tor, where have you been? I yam crushed you haven't come see me." She stroked his head with her antennas. "Such a naughty boy to abandon your Consuela."

"My schedule…very busy…"

Vanessa Painted Lady fluttered her way up to him, her reddish-orange wings stroking him on the head. "I can't sing a note without your cough drops." The eyes on her wings stared at him sadly.

"Hopper," said Mantis, coldly, "I remind you the game is afoot."

"Sorry, Mantis. Professional commitments, you know." He was backing away from the ladies. "I'll see you all very soon on my rounds."

Boring Beetle watched them fly away. "I say, Doctor, you have a bewitching clientele."

"Yes," admitted Hopper. "A significant portion of my patients are in the theatrical profession."

"Because you spend most of your evenings in their dressing rooms," said Mantis.

"Now, Mantis, you know it's only the odd occasion when I go backstage."

"You send fudge and flowers nightly."

"An exaggeration surely."

Mantis signaled for a carriage and the four bugs climbed in. "Mine Town, quick as you can," called Mantis up to the driver.

The whip cracked and two large horseflies answered the whip with a burst of speed that caused Hopper to grip his hat as he fell back in his seat. They were rolling.

Adora Ant sat next to Boring Beetle but addressed all three of her champions. "I appreciate what you're doing for me, sirs."

They were rolling.

"A puzzle is what we like," said Boring Beetle, "and you've given us a dandy one, eh Mantis?"

But Mantis only stared out the window, his long arms folded, an unlit pipe clenched in his mouth.

"Lost in thought," said Boring Beetle. "Reminds me of a chap I knew lived inside a leaf. Had no legs as it turns out, but he was able to glue together two halves of any leaf and make a cozy little retreat for himself. Couldn't get a word out of him. Hermit, you see. And deep. What passed through his mind when he was rolled up inside his leaf may well have been the key to the universe but we'll never know because, like Mantis here, you couldn't get a word out of him." Boring Beetle drew out a cigar. "Does anyone mind if I smoke?"

No one minded, as they were all asleep, including Mantis.

"Tired," said Boring Beetle to himself. "I see a lot of it. Comes from poor diet, I suspect. Saps the strength." He lit his cigar and smoked contentedly until the driver of the cab called out, "Mine Town!"

The other bugs woke with a jolt, Mantis staring at the tip of a burning cigar and cursing himself for having fallen asleep. He stepped from the carriage. One glance at the street told him he was going to need a clear head.

Mining beetles swaggered around, knives in their belts. Some sported pistols, a few carried rifles. They shouted, sang raucous songs, and drank cheap nectar out of filthy bottles. Dance halls and saloons had their doors wide open, catering to the beetles after their day in the mines.

Horseflies were tethered to hitching posts along the street, saddles on their backs, picks, shovels, and other mining gear attached. The Chief Constable's office had bullet holes in the door and windows; a faded wanted poster had a knife stuck in it. The interior of the office was empty and covered with dust.

"There is no law here," said Mantis.

Doctor Hopper was feeling for his own pistol, tucked in an inside

jacket pocket designed for it. He'd had it since his Army days when
he was a young doctor serving in Lettuce Land where he'd been
badly wounded, an assassin bug's bullet grazing the ventral ganglia
and ending his military career. "What's our next move, Mantis?"

"Miss Adora Ant will determine that," answered Mantis. He
turned to that lady. "Your assailant is here somewhere. Using you,
we shall draw him out."

"Using me?" she asked uneasily.

Hopper explained more gently. "He means, my dear, that you will
probably be rendered unconscious by the Invisible Hand."

"Oh no!"

"But we shall be there. You have nothing to fear."

"But it ain't very nice, being knocked out."

Doctor Hopper was distracted by a pair of orange wings.

"Come on in, boys. The show starts in five minutes." It was a
painted lady, calling to them from the doorway of a dance hall.

"Just the ticket, eh Mantis? Mingle with the crowd, have a drop of nectar?"

"Very well, Doctor, lead on."

Inside, beetles danced badly with painted ladies, twisting them around the floor to the music of a tinny piano played by a centipede whose hundred arms were all over the keyboard. He sang as he played a fast favorite, Jumping Bedbugs.

Around the edges of the dance floor miners gambled with cards and dice. Some had their pistols lying on the table beside them; others had already used theirs, for bullet holes filled the walls. Silk webs hung from the ceiling, smoke drifting through the threads. Here and there a spider could be seen crawling overhead, carrying trays of nectar to the balcony, where couples were engaged in private conversation.

"A vile deathtrap," said Boring Beetle, looking around the dance hall. "But stimulating. Puts one on one's toes."

A drunken miner elbowed his way roughly past them. Adora Ant, whose nerves were on edge, snapped at him with her mandibles. The miner spun around, knife drawn.

"Sheathe your knife," said Mantis, stepping between them.

The miner squinted at Mantis. "Who the blazes are you to tell me what to do?"

"I am the last thing you'll see in this life," said Mantis, calmly, "unless you do as I say." His great long arms opened just slightly, revealing the deadly sharp spines growing out of them. "You have one knife, I have many."

The miner studied the gleaming points arrayed against him. "Another time maybe," he said, backing away.

"Any time you like." Mantis's head suddenly swiveled completely around, so fast it was a blur.

A scorpion stood behind him, poisonous tail raised. Mantis moved slowly, waiting for the strike.

Boring Beetle had begun conversation with a masked bedbug hunter. "Bedbugs are conspicuously absent from this dance hall, sir, and I

"Come on in, boys. The show starts in five minutes."

attribute it to your presence. You stalk, you pounce, you kill. Were I a
bedbug I would be elsewhere myself. Your mask, by the way, interests
me greatly. Sticky hairs covered with dust and other particles, is it not?"

The bedbug hunter fell to the floor, instantly bored into unconsciousness, beside the scorpion who had also collapsed.

"Drunk," said Boring Beetle to Mantis. "Both of them. Can't hold
their nectar."

Mantis relaxed his guard. "You're a handy fellow to have around,
Boring Beetle."

Boring Beetle's long antennas waved back and forth in the air.
"Dashed amount of perfume in the air, makes one dizzy. All these
painted ladies, pouring out their attractants. Miners are helpless
against it. Look at them, spending their hard-earned gold on a dance."

The miners careened around the floor, painted ladies in their
arms, the eyes of the ladies distant, dreaming of the day they could
earn enough money to get away. "But of course, it will never come.
They'll be dancing here till they die."

"Harsh words, Boring Beetle," said Doctor Hopper, sympathetic
to the painted ladies' plight.

"Hard truth, Doctor. I've seen it in mining towns from here to the Valley of the Black Gnats. I loved a painted lady there and she took me for every penny I had. I was young of course. I know better now. Beautiful wings are not everything."

As Boring Beetle elaborated on his early love, dancers were falling, bored through the brain by the droning voice at the edge of the dance floor.

"And that is how they wind up in the end," said Boring Beetle, pointing to a group of hag moths seated alone at a table. "Their beauty gone, they no longer dance. I don't dare look too closely. My old love might be among them."

At which point, the manager of the dance hall came over to them and spoke bluntly to Boring Beetle. "I'm going to have to ask you to leave, laddie. You're knocking out all my customers."

"Rubbish," said Boring Beetle. "You just sold them too much nectar. Moderation in everything, that's the secret."

"And that's the door," said the manager. "Let's have no trouble."

"Come along, Boring Beetle," said Hopper. "The song we want to hear isn't being sung in this place."

"Very well," said Boring Beetle. "We'll take our business else-where." With a dismissive wave of his antennas, he led the way across the dance floor, stepping over unconscious dancers, min-ing beetles and painted ladies deep in sleep. Nearby gamblers had collapsed head down on their tables.

"And don't come back," said the manager as they left the dance hall.

They walked along the street past the hitching posts and rails. The horseflies stamped their feet and buzzed their wings sleepily. A cart with a barrel on it advertised Fresh Nectar.

"You should eat again, Miss Adora," said Doctor Hopper. "You need your strength for what lies ahead."

The owner of the cart was a filthy kissing bug, his lips stained with a vile juice. He sang to himself as he chewed a dark leaf and scratched his stomach lazily.

"A cup of nectar for this young lady," said Hopper.

"Drawn straight from the barrel," said the kissing bug, and he did just that. "Doesn't get any fresher." He handed the cup to Adora. "You folks are new in town. You'll find it a quiet little place."

Gunshots were sounding on the other side of street. "Far from the noise and cares of the big city," continued the kissing bug, as a flaming arrow whizzed past his head. "I've been here many years without a spot of trouble." Two staghorn beetles fell off the wooden sidewalk into the street, swinging at each other with enormous

pincers, clacking and snapping and removing the lower half of the kissing bug's mustache. "And if it's entertainment you want, take your pick." He pointed to the row of saloons.

Adora Ant had a mouth full of nectar. A high pitched sound filled the air. Her mouth fell open, and a spectral figure, moving at a tremendous rate of speed, descended on her and in one second drained her nectar and was gone.

Hopper's pistol was out but it was too late.

Adora Ant remained as she was, mouth open, body frozen. Hopper administered a stimulant, bringing her quickly around.

"The Invisible Hand," she cried. "It got me again."

"There, there," said Hopper, consoling her. "You're perfectly all right."

"I ain't perfectly all right," said Adora. "I been robbed." She pointed inside her empty mouth.

In tones void of feeling, Mantis remarked, "That was a most remarkable display."

"Quite," said Boring Beetle, with equal calm. "A daring attack."

"It's the sound of the wings that renders her catatonic," said Mantis.

"I say, Mantis, Miss Adora has had a terrible shock." Hopper was holding the hand of Adora Ant. "And we were supposed to prevent it."

"Preventing it wasn't possible. The creature moved too quickly."

"I think," continued Hopper, "you might show a bit of sympathy."

Mantis appeared not to know what Hopper was talking about, and Hopper could only reflect that Mantis was sadly lacking in decent feeling. But that was the price of a brilliant intellect, the feelings were crushed into insignificance. He attempted to make up for Mantis's failure. "Miss Adora, don't lose faith in us. We're sadly grieved that you had to endure yet another assault."

The poor ant gazed at him with her big eyes. "You're all I've got," she said.

"You've got me," said the filthy kissing bug, wriggling his body in an inappropriate way. "How's about a little kiss?"

Adora Ant drew back and Hopper intervened. "That's enough of that."

"It's my nature," said the kissing bug. "I can't help it."

"Just give the young lady another cup of nectar."

"Pay up first, that's the friendly way."

Hopper paid and Miss Adora put the cup to her lips. Far overhead the whining sound was heard. But it came no closer.

"It won't risk another attack just yet," said Mantis, studying the dark sky. He turned to Adora Ant. "You may drink without fear of interruption."

Adora Ant did just that but her anxiety had not lessened.

"What's puzzling," said Hopper, "is why the Invisible Hand doesn't suck nectar out of this fellow's barrel."

At that moment, a cockroach ambling along the street changed direction abruptly and made a rush at the nectar barrel.

The kissing bug whipped out a shotgun and fired at the cockroach, who flew into the air with buckshot holes in its wings. The kissing bug reloaded. "As I said earlier, this is the friendliest little town you'll find for many a mile. With goodwill and understanding, that's how we get along here."

"You shot holes in the wings of that roach," said Hopper.

"A town like this provides happy memories, souvenirs of warm fellowship that last a lifetime."

"And I believe one of its legs was blown off."

"He'll grow a new one and thank me for it. That's how we do things here." The kissing bug stowed the shotgun, having answered the question of why the Invisible Hand didn't steal from him. "More nectar, anyone?"

Hopper would've liked some, but Mantis was growing impatient. "The fiend has toyed with us," he said. "And I am not amused."

"Quite. Your reputation and all that," said Hopper. "But a last little nip of nectar surely won't tarnish your reputation any further."

"Have your nip, Doctor." Mantis was scanning the buildings that lined the street.

The kissing bug poured for Hopper. "Your friend thinks he can catch the Invisible Hand."

"He does."

"Can't be done."

"You seem remarkably sure of yourself."

The kissing bug nodded toward Adora Ant. "We get aphid herders like her coming through here from time to time. The Invisible Hand eats their lunch. They barely have strength to get out of town."

"You've seen this happen?"

"Ants frozen, mouth open? Sure, we all see it. Quite funny actually."

"You shot holes in the wings of that roach"

"Not for the ants."

"When they come to, they always have the same dumb look on their face." The kissing bug chuckled. "Some of them never snap out of it. They just topple over. Very entertaining. Part of the charm of this place."

"Do they die?" asked Adora Ant in a quavering voice.

"And we drag them away. Dried up, stiff. Mouth still open. Funniest thing you ever saw."

Adora Ant had turned pale.

The kissing bug looked at her curiously. "Something I said?"

Boring Beetle took the arm of Adora Ant. "Come along, Miss Adora." And he moved her down the dusty street, with Hopper and Mantis coming along behind them.

The sun was setting. In the doorway of the Firefly Hotel and Casino, a firefly flashed her light through the flimsy material of her casino costume. "Come on in, boys. Play a hand of cards."

"Here as anywhere," said Mantis, nodding to the doorway of the Firefly Saloon.

Hopper counseled Boring Beetle. "If you don't mind, old man, I think it would be better if you said as little as possible when we get inside."

"Secrecy, eh? By all means. When I traveled with Sir Julius Squash

Bug to the Empire of the Tiger Beetles, we communicated entirely by a series of feigned hiccups. Worked rather well until…"

The firefly in the doorway of the saloon fell backward, instantly bored into unconsciousness. Hopper hurried to catch her.

Her eyes opened slowly. "What happened?"

"Don't worry, I'm a doctor." Hopper stroked her forehead gently

as he said softly, "You were bored into unconsciousness. But you're perfectly sound and healthy."

"Come along, Hopper," said Mantis, pushing past them.

"I'll be inside, Miss, should you require further assistance."

The Firefly Casino possessed a tiny stage, empty at the moment. Card tables filled the saloon and numerous games were in progress. Mantis and his party lined up at the bar, Mantis leaning back on it with his long arms, in order to scan the casino.

"What'll it be, folks?" asked a vinegar fly, wiping down the bar in front of them with a dirty rag.

"Your best rosewater," said Hopper.

When they were served, Boring Beetle lifted his glass. "I should like to give a lengthy toast but will refrain. Mum's the word."

The four bugs clicked their glasses.

From around the casino came the sound of cards being shuffled by six-armed dealers. To this was added the clicking of a spinning roulette wheel, and the rattle of dice. Everywhere bugs were gambling, most of them mining beetles but there were other bugs and even a deadly-looking spider.

"Lycosidae," said Mantis. "The wolf spider, a very dangerous character. Chases down its victims, bites once, and all is over."

"And here it sits," said Hopper, "a murderer freely interacting with hard-working bugs."

"In a town without law," said Mantis, "a murderer is free to do as he likes."

"I wouldn't want to be playing cards with the fellow," said Hopper, "although that round little pill bug across from him seems confident enough."

"That is not a pill bug," said Mantis. "It is the coiling millipede, Glomeris marginata."

"Half the size of the spider and totally unconcerned from the look of it."

At which point the spider slammed down his cards and shouted, "You cheating little pill!"

"He has mistaken his opponent," said Mantis. "A common error."

The spider leapt across the table and attacked the little millipede, who immediately coiled up into something resembling a pill. A bright secretion appeared on its coiled form, and the spider jumped back. "You disgusting runt, you got your filth on me." The spider wiped the secretion off his hairy arms.

The coiled millipede chuckled quietly while remaining tucked into a ball.

The wolf spider moved away, still rubbing his arms. "Loathsome wretch. He can have his winnings. I wouldn't touch anything he's touched."

"A wise idea," said Mantis, softly to Hopper, "but I'm afraid it's too late."

The spider stood at the bar and ordered a drink.

"In a town without law," said Mantis, "a murderer is free to do as he likes."

"Bit of a scrape, no harm done," said the vinegar fly, wiping the bar with his dirty rag and then serving the spider.

The spider raised the drink, still watching the round little millipede who had now uncoiled and was once again sitting upright.

"You're repulsive," shouted the spider.

The little millipede only grinned.

Suddenly the spider twitched spasmodically and fell to the floor.

Doctor Hopper quickly opened his medical bag but Mantis placed a hand on the bag. "There's nothing you can do. The spider has played his last hand of cards. He was dead the moment he touched the millipede."

Hopper knelt over the spider and cautiously sniffed. "You're right, Mantis. It's quinazolinone poisoning."

"Our friend over there—" Mantis nodded toward the grinning millipede. "—secretes it from eight mid-dorsal pores. A most effective distribution system. Anywhere you grab him is deadly."

Mining beetles were crowding around the body. "Stiff already," said one of them.

They turned toward the millipede, and another of them said, "That's one tough little bug."

Two waiters came over, picked up the spider, and tossed him out the back door. The games of chance resumed, no one seeming to care very much about the demise of the spider.

But Boring Beetle's antennas were working furiously. He could contain himself no longer. "We're being watched, Mantis. Someone has taken a keen interest in our movements. I can feel their intention."

"Is it the Invisible Hand?"

"Or his minions."

Their exchange was interrupted by a drum roll announcing further entertainment. A disheveled master of ceremonies bounced onstage. "And now, ladies and gentlemen, direct from the capital of Bugland, the world famous hypnotist, Alexander Apple Worm!"

The hypnotist came on stage, dressed in a battered top hat and frayed tuxedo. He removed the top hat as he bowed to the audience. "I shall need a volunteer. You, sir." He pointed to a mining beetle.

"I can't be hypnotized, be a waste of time."

"Is that so?" Alexander Apple Worm made a slight gesture. "And when did you begin your career as a ballet dancer?"

At first the mining beetle looked confused. Then he said, "I don't remember when. I been at it a long time."

"You'd like to show us a few steps, wouldn't you? That's if your contract permits you. You are with the Bugland Ballet, aren't you?"

The mining beetle began a clumsy display, his steps forced by gestures from Alexander Apple Worm; the miner kicked awkwardly with his several legs, stumbling against tables and finally crashing into the stage and upending himself, to the great delight of his friends.

"A brilliant dancing display," said the hypnotist. "Let's have a big hand for the star of the Bugland Ballet."

The crowd applauded and the mining beetle got to his feet, once again confused. "What happened?"

"Come on back here and sit down, Bob," said his friends, and guided him to the table where he sat down heavily. "That's it, Bob, you take 'er easy, you been dancin' to beat the band."

"Seems like I was thrashin' around. But it's all a blur."

"Don't worry about it." His friends patted him on the back. "You got a whole new career ahead of you." And they roared with laughter and stamped their feet under the table in imitation of Bob.

Alexander Apple Worm hypnotized dozens of other bugs, making them believe they were trapeze artists, opera singers, and even caused one bug to believe he was a slice of cheese.

At the end of the act, Apple Worm took a few bows and vanished backstage. Mantis found a small staircase at the side of the stage and with the others in his party followed Apple Worm into a shabby dressing room.

"We enjoyed your performance, Mr. Apple Worm," said Mantis.

"This town is a dump, sir," said Apple Worm. "But I, who once performed for the Empress Moth of Bugland, have fallen on hard times." He took a flask from his pocket. "Drink, my curse." He looked at Adora Ant. "Forgive me, miss, while I indulge."

After a few swigs from his flask, he gazed into a broken dressing room mirror. "I can hypnotize them into believing they're toadstools. One would think I could hypnotize myself into leading a decent life."

"Let's have a big hand for the star of the Bugland Ballet."

He polished the flask with his sleeve. "But there you have it, a ruined bug, forced to play broken-down holes like this." At which point, the leg of his chair broke underneath him and he collapsed on the floor.

"I'll sue them," he said, struggling to his feet.

"But you are the greatest hypnotist in Bugland," said Mantis.

Apple Worm clutched the back of the broken chair. "Kind of you to say so, sir."

"With one exception."

Alexander Apple Worm frowned. "There are no exceptions, sir."

"He's called the Invisible Hand."

"An amateur. Very limited in his scope." Apple Worm peered at himself in the mirror again as if hoping for a better reflection. "He has one trick and one only."

"You've seen him in action?"

"No one sees him, sir."

"Yet you call him an amateur."

"I do." He gestured toward Adora and made a humming sound. Her mouth fell open. "Is this a trick worthy of the name?" He gestured again and Adora Ant's mouth closed back up. "She is highly suggestible. Every ant of her type has the same weakness. The Invisible Hand takes advantage of it. I see no great talent in that."

Boring Beetle was dying to say something but kept his promise to be quiet. His antennas however were moving with agitation.

Mantis asked Apple Worm, "Are you aware of any weakness the Invisible Hand may have?"

"Pride, sir. A common failing in those with some little gift."

"How do you know about his pride?"

"One gets a feeling for these things. To give but one example, he loves to strike when visiting dignitaries come to town, and after striking he takes cover in the clouds, but continues his signature whine so all will know he's there. I could go on."

"That won't be necessary," said Mantis, and to Doctor Hopper's great surprise turned to Boring Beetle.

"Boring Beetle, you were speaking of your travels with Sir Julius Squash Bug. I should very much like to hear a bit more."

Boring Beetle snapped to attention. "Happy to oblige, Mantis. Sir Julius and I were deep in Tiger Beetle territory. The Tiger larvas lurked in the sand, just their powerful jaws disguised as twigs. One misstep and they'd have your leg off. The adult Tigers were no better. They roamed by night seeking their prey. You'd see an iridescent green figure moving stealthily if you saw him at all. The next thing you knew he'd be at your throat. Did I say he stank to high heaven? A foul-smelling secretion was part of his defense. Along with a smokescreen blown from his nether parts. I tell you it was hard going."

Doctor Hopper and Adora Ant along with Alexander Apple Worm were driven into unconsciousness by Boring Beetle. Mantis had fought against it and now struggled to the door. He yanked it open and found a spy unconscious in the hallway. "You were right, Boring Beetle." They hurried to the next dressing room and found another spy, unconscious against the hole in the wall he'd been peering through.

"Sleeping on the job," said Boring Beetle. "I see a lot of that."

Mantis, now confident that no one could be listening to his next move, hurried back to the hypnotist's dressing room. He shook Adora Ant and Alexander Apple Worm awake, saying urgently to Apple Worm, "I have no time for explanations. You must show your greater power, greater than the Invisible Hand. You must hypnotize Miss Adora Ant, giving her the autosuggestion that she will not, I repeat not succumb to the sound of the Invisible Hand. Can you do that?"

"Do it? It's done, sir." He turned to Adora Ant, said, "Sleep now," and instantly her head fell forward. He put his lips beside her ear and whispered, "You hear only my words. Nothing else. In all the world there only my words. Nod your head if you understand."

She nodded.

He implanted the command and turned to Mantis. "She's blockaded, sir, as you wished." He turned back to Adora Ant. "On the count of three you will awake, refreshed and restored." He gave the count and Adora Ant woke with a smile.

"I've had a lovely dream."

Doctor Hopper woke at the same time and was pleased to see her smiling. Was her ordeal almost over? The question had to go unanswered for the moment.

The door to the dressing room opened and a waiter announced, "They're calling for you, Al."

Alexander Apple Worm applied a brush to the brim of his top hat, then straightened the threadbare cuffs of his tuxedo jacket. "My costume is unraveling, as am I. But—" He slapped his top hat on. "—I can still fool an audience."

"Your show is excellent," said Hopper.

"I'll turn the lot of them into barstools," said Apple Worm. And saying which, he departed the dressing room.

"What now, Mantis?" asked Hopper.

"We take rooms here. I've come to like the establishment."

Hopper didn't protest. He knew that Mantis had formed a plan and staying in the Firefly Hotel and Casino was part of it.

He yanked it open and found a spy unconscious in the hallway.

A BEDBUG MANAGED the hotel rooms for the casino. "Here's a perfect room for the little lady." The wallpaper was peeling, the only chair was broken, and the bed was rusty.

"It's very nice," said Adora Ant who had never slept away from home before.

"As requested," said the bedbug to Hopper, "you bugs have suitably furnished rooms on each side of her."

"Yes, these will do," said Hopper.

"Call if you need anything," said the bedbug. "I'm always at the end of the hall."

Mantis instructed Adora Ant to stay in her room until they called for her in the morning. "One of us will always be outside your door and watching. You have nothing to fear."

"You said that before."

"Hopper, give her your pistol."

Hopper showed her how to use it.

Mantis took the chair from her room and placed it outside her door. "We won't fail you," he said, and crossed his long arms, the knifelike daggers showing.

"Then, good night," said Adora Ant and closed the door. "They mean well," she said to herself. She lay down on the bed and put the pistol under her pillow. It had been a very long day. In seconds she was asleep.

Outside her room, Mantis watched. From the end of the hallway, the bedbug watched him. Mantis went to Boring Beetle's room. "Boring Beetle, would you go down the hall and tell the bedbug about the Empire of the Tiger Beetles?"

"He wishes to increase his knowledge? Admirable." Boring Beetle marched to the end of the hallway and spoke at length to the bedbug. The bedbug slipped out of his chair and fell on the floor. He was still unconscious when Hopper came out to relieve Mantis at two in the morning.

Mantis went into their room and flung himself on the bed. He slept fitfully for he was still revolving his plan. But slowly the pieces sifted into place and by dawn he was ready.

"THIS WILL BE OUR OPPORTUNITY." Mantis spoke to the other bugs over breakfast, and pointed to a newspaper headline.

Mine Town On Rails!

"The tracks to Mine Town are being laid at this moment," said Mantis. "The first train will arrive at noon. The president of Bugland Railway will be on it, along with other dignitaries."

Boring Beetle was alert to the implication. "Alexander Apple Worm said the Invisible Hand—"

"—attacks when dignitaries are around."

" I don't want nobody attacking me," said Adora Ant.

"The attack will fail," said Mantis.

"I'm glad you think so."

Hopper noticed a waiter edging closer for no good reason. Stealing himself against what was to come, Hopper asked Boring Beetle, "Were you captured by the Tiger Beetles?"

"Indeed we were. Imagine a pit writhing with hungry larvas. I don't have to imagine it as the sight is forever engraved in my mind. Those hideous white bodies, those snapping pincers, those open mouths."

The waiter collapsed en route to the table, bored to the floor by Boring Beetle. Boring Beetle glanced at him. "Drunk already? Disgraceful. Shall I complain to the management?"

"Let sleeping dogs lie," said Mantis. "We can now speak more freely."

"Ah, quite. Point taken." Boring Beetle got up and helped himself to more jam. "We have no need of the fellow anyway." He sat down with fresh jam and toast. "You were saying, Mantis?"

"After the president of Bugland Rail addresses the crowd, entertainment will commence." He pointed to the newspaper again. "A marching band will play. Doctor Hopper, you will accompany Miss Adora Ant on the fiddle."

The lady in question had been rendered unconscious by Boring Beetle and they let her rest, for she'd complained that owing to her fears she'd slept badly.

"We shall have to practice," said Hopper.

"One song will be sufficient."

"Bug of My Dreams is always a crowd pleaser."

"Then Bug of My Dreams it will be."

"She has a sweet voice," said Hopper. "But I shall have to find a fiddle." He rose from the table. "I'd best begin my search."

Hopper stepped over the unconscious waiter and walked up Main Street. Before long he came to the Pigeon Louse Pawnshop. Hanging in the window were a number of musical instruments. He entered to the ringing of a bell above the door. The pigeon louse came forward to greet him. "You're up early, sir."

"I wish to buy a fiddle."

"So you may fiddle away the day. Good, excellent. I have several fine instruments. This one here—" He reached up to where guitars, banjos, and fiddles hung. "—was owned by a cricket like yourself. Played in the town square at night. Two of the firefly ladies used to come around and light up for him."

"And where is he now?"

"Deceased, sir. A victim of fiddling, you might say."

"I don't understand."

"Well, he fiddled for both of the firefly ladies. And he couldn't make up his mind which one was the light of his life. So one of the fireflies shot him."

"Good heavens."

"Fireflies have that hot light in them."

"Luciferin," said Hopper, familiar with it from his medical practice.

"Fiona Firefly had a bit too much of it I guess. Took out a pistol and drilled him while he was singing to her rival." The pigeon louse handed the fiddle to Hopper. "Handcarved, high gloss, inlaid with mother-of-bug. A very distinctive instrument."

"Let sleeping dogs lie," said Mantis.

Hopper tuned it up. The sound was mellow. "He was playing this—?"

"—when she drilled him."

"I'm not superstitious but—"

"That's why I'm going to let you have it for half price."

Hopper looked at the tag. A remarkable bargain.

The pigeon louse said, "Musicians leave a bit of their soul in an instrument."

Hopper ran the bow over the strings again. They did seem to sing with a special quality, sad but sweet. Like Miss Adora Ant herself. "Very well, I'll take it."

"You've made a wise decision, sir. The instrument will repay you many times over." The pigeon louse took out a case and opened it. Inside, sewn into the plush lining was the name Conway Cricket.

"As fine a fiddler as you'd ever want to hear. But naïve when it came to fireflies."

Hopper laid the fiddle into the case and snapped it shut. He paid the pigeon louse. The bell over the door tinkled once again as he left the pawnshop. "Conway Cricket played in the town square and that is where I'll practice," said Hopper, and headed along the street toward the square.

It was in no way grand, just trees and benches around a small fountain. It was empty at this early hour and Hopper had a bench to himself. He opened the case and brought out the fiddle. "A handsome instrument," he said, and tucked it under his chin. Then he noticed a sheet of paper inside the case. "Conway Cricket's playlist." He scanned the list and saw that he knew several of the songs. He began playing the Warble Fly Waltz which had a nice old feeling. He followed this with Lullaby of the Louse, then You Give Me A Buzz. He lost himself in the music and not until he played Deep in the Heart of Bugland did he realize he had an audience.

A firefly, a very attractive one, was looking at him with tears in her eyes. She said through her tears, "I couldn't believe it when I heard you. I thought, it's Conway come back from the grave."

"I'm afraid it's only his fiddle come back from the pawnshop."

The firefly came closer, saw the name Conway Cricket inside the case and sat down, sobbing.

"Please, please," said Hopper, handing her his handkerchief. "Dry your tears."

"They'll never be dry." She gave him a dramatic look. He could not help but feel she was in the theatrical profession.

"I take it you are not the one who shot him?"

"I loved him. He was my life." She said this with an even more dramatic expression.

"But you didn't shoot him?"

"My love burned brightly. Too brightly." She put one hand to her heart, the other to her brow and turned dramatically toward the morning sun. "Can the sun stop shining? Can a firefly stop loving?"

Hopper wanted to be perfectly clear on one point. "But the shooting business, that wasn't you."

"A gun went off. I looked and saw it in my hand, the barrel smoking."

Hopper began packing Conway Cricket's fiddle away, keeping a careful eye on Fiona Firefly. She'd killed one fiddler. She might easily kill another.

"Where are you going?" she demanded.

"I have urgent business to attend to."

"Stay where you are." A pistol, presumably the one fired at Conway Cricket, was pointed at Hopper. "Play Warble Fly Waltz again."

Hopper, having given his own pistol to Adora Ant, had no choice but to take the fiddle back out of the case and resume playing.

Fiona Firefly said, "If I close my eyes, you could be Conway."

"I assure you, miss, I'm not Conway."

"No, there was no one like him. One of a kind, that was Conway."

Hopper continued playing in the style of one-of-a-kind Conway, the pistol pointed straight at his head. *How do I get myself into these situations?* He watched for an opportunity to hop away. *Two good leaps and he'd clear the fountain.*

"I'm an excellent shot," she said.

Perhaps two leaps would not be sufficient.

Fiona Firefly raised her arms to the sky. "Oh Conway, why did you have to cheat on me?"

More dramatic gestures, this time with a pistol.

"You sang love songs to me, then snuck off with her."

The pistol whipped dramatically past Hopper's mustache.

"Dear lady, I beg you…"

"Don't stop playing. Never stop playing."

"Never?"

"When you play I'm with him again. Time is turned backward."

Perhaps if I leaped backward, over the bench, then kicked strongly, cleared the sidewalk and landed in the trees…

"Play on. I must hear more of dear Conway's song."

Hopper continued playing the Warble Fly Waltz, and Fiona kept time to the music by waving her pistol. Hopper could imagine better ways of conducting the tune but was reluctant to suggest them.

Then he saw a flashing light moving along behind the bushes and suddenly another female firefly was standing in front of them. "Put that pistol away, you idiot," she said, "before you kill some-one else."

"Play Warble Fly Waltz again."

Fiona Firefly pointed the pistol at her rival. "I should've shot you, not Conway."

Hopper lowered his fiddle. I'll just take this opportunity to slip away…

The pistol whipped around toward him. "Don't move."

Hopper froze.

"Keep playing."

He kept playing. The newest firefly said to him, "Are you going to let this lunatic—" She pointed at Fiona." —tell you what to do?"

"Under the circumstances, I'm inclined to."

"You're kind of cute. Not as cute as Conway, of course."

This Conway Cricket, reflected Hopper, seems to have been a remarkable specimen.

"But you'll do."

"Excuse me?"

"You're a fiddler, aren't you?"

"I fiddle a bit, but—"

She twisted the pistol out of Fiona's grip. "You go home and take a cold shower." She turned to Hopper. "And you come with me."

"Why?"

"Because I have the pistol."

The statement carried a certain weight, so Hopper packed his fiddle, tipped his hat to Fiona, and said, "I'll be leaving now. I suggest you forget Conway Cricket."

"I was the light of his life." Fiona pointed scornfully toward the other firefly. "She was just a spark in the dark."

The situation has become complicated, said Hopper to himself. But my direction seems clear. I'll follow the other firefly, then make a dash for freedom.

She said, "I need a fiddler at my restaurant. My customers like music while they dine."

"I'm grateful for the offer of employment but—"

"I've got the pistol. Or had you forgotten?"

"Do you hold all of your employees at gunpoint?"

"When I have to." They were now walking along Main Street. "Conway worked for me until Fiona shot him. He created a romantic atmosphere. Candlelight, nectar wine, and Conway Cricket's fiddle."

Hopper protested, "The fiddle is just a hobby of mine. I don't have a large repertoire."

"You were playing the Warble Fly Waltz. That's good enough."

"Your customers will want more."

"You'll learn more."

These fireflies are demanding creatures, reflected Hopper. He glanced at a horsefly tied to a nearby hitching post. I could leap onto that beast and ride fervently away.

"Don't try it."

Telepathic too.

He tried a different angle. "I'm afraid there's been a misunderstanding. My profession is that of medical doctor."

"When someone is shot in my restaurant you can provide immediate attention."

"Is being shot a usual part of the dining experience there?"

"It comes with the entrée."

They crossed Main Street and she pointed with her pistol to a restaurant called Eats.

Hopper observed, "A modest sign."

"In this town you don't need much." She prodded him in the back with her pistol. "Inside, Doc."

As it was morning, the restaurant was empty except for a couple of houseflies sweeping up. "Boys, this is Doc. Our new fiddler."

"Looks like Conway."

Saying which, the houseflies resumed sweeping up broken bottles, cigar butts, match flaps, and soggy sawdust. A Conway look-alike meant little to them.

"You'll sit over here." The firefly led Hopper to a stool in the corner. "That way the customers will get a good look at you. You can start practicing now."

Hopper took out his fiddle and began to play Moth to the Flame.

"Beautiful," said the firefly. "Tugs at the heart." She sat down at a nearby table and laid the pistol in front of her. "They're going to love you."

The door to the restaurant opened and Boring Beetle entered with Adora Ant. "Ah, Hopper, there you are. We thought we'd lost you."

"Who are you?" demanded the firefly.

"Broderick Boring Beetle, at your service." Antennas waving, he performed an elegant bow, then noticed the firearm in front of her on the table. "I see you like the Slingerland Six-shot. I used it myself while searching for the legendary Bigfoot Fly. It was harsh country and we were attacked by crab spiders, so named because of their habit of running sideways. They spin no snare but wait inside a flower, ready to pounce. Numbers of them came at us at once and I can tell you I was glad to have the repeating firepower of the Slingerland pistol."

The firefly's head was on the table. Both houseflies were unconscious on the floor. "Boring Beetle, thank heavens you came. I was being held here against my will."

"We can't have that, old man. You're needed for the celebration." Boring Beetle picked up the Slingerland pistol. "I'd better keep this."

"Boys, this is Doc. Our new fiddler."

They hurried out of the restaurant. Hopper said to Adora, "We've got to find a safe place to rehearse."

"It's taken care of," said Boring Beetle. "Chap I met has just the thing."

Boring Beetle led them to a tunnel where a mining beetle await-ed them. "Calls himself Skipjack. Rough sort but cooperative."

Skipjack was chewing juicy leaves and spitting. He looked them up and down. "Fancy clothes for a mine," he said, a note of scorn in his voice.

"Let us worry about that, Mr. Skipjack," said Boring Beetle, who had investigated some treacherous caverns in his day, wearing then as he wore now a beautifully tailored suit.

"Suit yourself," said Skipjack, and lighting a lantern led the way into the mine.

Hopper and Adora followed the dancing light and the sounds of Skipjack's expectoration.

Finally they came to a small room excavated in the tunnel wall. "You want private, you got private," said Skipjack. "This mine's played out. Nobody comes down no more."

Boring Beetle paid him. Skipjack looked at the payment and said, "This is too much."

"I've given you a little something extra for I'm reminded of the last mine I was in, which brought me luck. You've heard of King Calopteron?"

"Can't say I have."

"Early warlord. For centuries it was believed his buried treasure was nothing but a legend. I felt otherwise. I had a map, I won't say from whom I got it, for reputations are involved, but the name would be familiar to you, I have no doubt on that score. Very well, map in hand we made our way up a pestilential river. I was accompanied by Prince Water Penny, minor royalty and in spite of his name penni-less, but the best bug I know for work of that sort. You've read his memoirs?"

The mining beetle had fallen with his head against the wall of the tunnel. His snores were muffled.

"Mine gas?" Boring Beetle waved his antennas. "I don't detect any. I think we're safe." He examined the mining beetle. "Played out, like his mine. Well, it's a hard life. We'll let him sleep, eh?"

Hopper retreated with Adora Ant into the excavated room, far enough to diminish the force of Boring Beetle's delivery. He took out his fiddle.

Boring Beetle called to him. "I'll just wait out here. You folks fill the air with melody."

Hopper asked Adora, "Do you know the words to Bug of My Dreams?"

Adora nodded. Hopper took out his fiddle and began to play. Adora's sweet voice filled the little room of stone. Boring Beetle waved his antennas to the music. Skipjack remained snoring against the wall.

Above ground, miners on their way to work heard the music and stopped.

"Comin' from that played-out hole," they said, and walked over to it. Other miners followed.

"That's as sweet a sound as I ever heard," said one of them.

"It ain't rough like what them gals sing at the saloons."

"Tender is what it is."

Then entered, swinging their lanterns and heading for the music.

"There's Skipjack. Looks like he's been took by the music."

Skipjack's head still rested against the tunnel wall.

"Skipjack always been sensitive."

Boring Beetle had not expected interruptions but he could see the miners were entranced by the voice of Adora Ant. And he remembered being similarly entranced, years ago in wild country, creeping through the bush, drawn by the song of a bewitching moth. She'd received him warmly. What memories! He couldn't very well refuse these fellows. He gave them a gesture of welcome with his long antennas.

Adora Ant sang and the miners listened appreciatively. There was something about the little ant's voice that touched them deeply. She'd fed her whole life on sweet aphid juice, it was in her veins and in her voice. When she finished Bug of My Dreams they applauded her and called for more.

She obliged them, for she knew many songs from singing to her aphids when they grew restless. Hopper improvised, the miners sang along. Skipjack awoke, said, "The walls have spoke to me." Carrying his lantern he marched on deeper into the mine.

"There goes Skipjack."

"Don't he know this mine is played out?"

"Always been a dreamer, old Skipjack."

The light of his lantern played on the walls of the mine as he descended. Suddenly a second shadow joined him, long and lean.

"Somebody else down there," said one of the miners.

"Another fool thinks there's gold left in this shaft."

The light from Skipjack's lantern faded. He was deep into the mine, with the other fool.

"They ain't going to strike nothing down there but hard rock."

"It's the music took them."

"It's pretty near took me." The beetle who said this had tears in his eyes and he wasn't the only one. More miners from above started drifting in. Soon the shaft was filled with beetles carrying picks and shovels, lanterns and lunch pails. Like Skipjack, they were rough around the edges but strangely quiet now, until Adora finished her song and they banged on their lunch pails, their highest form of tribute.

Adora Ant stared in wonder at the appreciative beetles. "Thank you," she said, sweetly and softly.

The miners, conferring among themselves, concluded, "She's the Angel of the Mines."

"Down here in the dark to show she cares."

And they urged her to sing on.

He could see the miners were entranced by the voice of Adora Ant.

Adora Ant sang and sang and Doctor Hopper found new facility on the fiddle. The hours passed quickly, and the concert might have gone on longer but the ground began to rumble.

"It's the new train come to town," observed a miner near the mouth of the tunnel. And the miners poured out to see the thing.

"That's our cue," said Hopper to Adora, and packed his fiddle.

"This way, my dear," said Boring Beetle, and gave her his arm.

Miners led the way for them with their lanterns. "Watch your step, miss. We don't want the Angel of the Mines getting hurt."

They reached the mouth of the tunnel and stepped back out into the light. Crowds of miners were moving through town toward the newly laid railroad tracks. A makeshift platform had been erected to greet the train carrying J. Emerson Earwig, president of Bugland Rail.

The train chugged into the station and Earwig stepped from the train onto the platform. The miners waved their shovels and cheered. Earwig lifted his top hat and waved it back at them in return. The miners liked that; some big shots wouldn't give a miner the time of day, When they stopped cheering he addressed them.

"Citizens, friends, Bugland Rail has heard your call." He went on with dull but heartfelt phrases.

"Where is Mantis?" Hopper asked Boring Beetle.

Once again the ground rumbled. But it was not from the train for the train was motionless beside the platform.

"It's coming from beneath our feet," said Boring Beetle. "Mining work of some kind, I daresay."

J. Emerson Earwig continued with his dull but heartfelt speech. Before he had finished it a blackened Skipjack came running up the street, hands in the air, clutching two glittering pieces of rock. "Gold! I struck gold!"

Walking slowly behind him was Inspector Mantis, also blackened with mine dust. He joined Hopper and Boring Beetle. "A controlled explosion, Hopper, made possible by my researches into the bombardier beetle, which you deemed worthless." With a blackened arm

he pointed toward Skipjack. "He used my explosion and is now rich beyond his wildest dreams."

"That second shadow in the shaft," said Boring Beetle.

"Mine," said Mantis.

"But how——?"

"——did I know there was gold? I confess I did not. But I had time on my hands while Hopper was rehearsing Miss Adora and decided to continue my experiment with the bombardier explosive." He looked at Hopper. "In a place where a bit of dust would bother no one. An abandoned mine shaft seemed perfect. Skipjack came along claiming the mine had spoken to him, that he knew just where to set off the blast."

"Mantis, that's all very well," said Hopper, "but I remind you we didn't come here to mine gold."

"Quite right. I think our real purpose will soon be realized."

The mayor of Mine Town was presenting J. Emerson Earwig with the key to the city. The town marching band played several numbers badly. The miners cheered and once again J. Emerson Earwig waved his top hat.

Then one of the miners called out, "Let the Angel of the Mines sing!"

"Yes, yes," answered the other miners.

"By all means," said J. Emerson Earwig.

"I second that," said the mayor.

"Come along, Miss Adora," said Hopper and led her toward the platform.

Boring Beetle thought to himself, All is going according to plan. Mantis is a clever fellow.

Hopper presented Adora to the president of Bugland Rail.

"The Angel of the Mines, eh?" J. Emerson Earwig reached into his vest pocket. "Please accept this lifetime pass on Bugland Rail with my compliments."

"Thank you, sir," said Adora. "I'll use it to visit my dear sisters."

"Bugland Rail will be honored to carry you there. And now you're going to sing a little song?"

"Bug of My Dreams, if you wish, sir."

"I wish it indeed. One of the old favorites."

Hopper stroked his fiddle and Adora Ant sang to J. Emerson Earwig and the crowd of miners. The miners saw the mine dust on her clothes. She was one of them and they loved her. Earwig hummed along, drumming his fingertips on his waistcoat.

Fiona Firefly worked her way through the crowd. For the past few hours she'd been indulging in nectar wine. To say she was not thinking clearly would be to understate the matter.

"Conway, you've cheated on me for the last time." She drew another pistol from her pocket and pointed it at Hopper.

A green scissor-like arm closed on her wrist.

"You don't want to do that," said Mantis.

"I've got her, sir," said a member of the marching band, who played the glockenspiel badly and had always had a crush on Fiona. He led the disoriented firefly away.

Adora Ant finished Bug of My Dreams.

"Beautifully rendered," said J. Emerson Earwig. He turned to the mayor. "Indeed she does have the voice of an angel."

"I propose a toast," said the mayor.

A bottle of nectar champagne was opened. The foaming drink was poured into three glasses. The miners cheered. Earwig, the mayor, and Adora Ant raised their glasses and drank.

The moment the nectar was in Adora's mouth a high-pitched sound from the sky was heard. A speeding figure descended on gleaming wings and hovered in front of Adora, expecting her mouth to open for him.

You hear only my words, said the voice of Alexander Apple Worm in her head. Her mouth did not open.

The crowd saw, for the first time, what the Invisible Hand looked like, his slender body in a beautifully tailored suit, his silvery wings humming, his proboscis like a bent straw as he waited for Adora's mouth to open.

"Why, it's a blamed mosquito," said one of the miners.

The Invisible Hand, perfectly visible now, increased the speed of his wings, thereby increasing the humming sound that should have transfixed Adora Ant and caused her mouth to open so he could drink through his bent straw.

You hear only my words, said the voice of Alexander Apple Worm.

"You're right," said another of the miners. "Nothing but a pesky mosquito."

The Invisible Hand, no longer invisible, still hovered in front of Adora. His eyes gleamed. Submit to me.

"You're just a mosquito," said Adora, swallowing her nectar champagne.

His suit was of silvery silk. His tie pin and cufflinks glittered. He was a fancy fellow, that was clear to the miners. They didn't like him.

"Get away from our Angel," shouted one of them.

"Sir," said J. Emerson Earwig, "you are interfering with the business of Bugland Rail."

Hovering in the air, the Invisible Hand rotated toward him. "And you are interfering with my lunch."

"I don't take your meaning, sir."

The Invisible Hand pointed his proboscis at Adora. "I drink from the mouths of ants."

"If that is true, it is a despicable habit."

Adora said, "You bet it is." Then she balled her fists up on her hips and thrust her head toward the silver-suited mosquito. "But you've had your last meal from me."

"So I failed to open your stupid mouth today. So what? Another opportunity will come."

This was too much for the miners. They were not going to stand for him talking like that to the Angel of the Mines. They started up the stairs after him.

"You must be joking," he said. He was too fast for a bunch of clumsy beetles. His wings hummed a high-pitched note as he said, "Eat my dust."

He sped off the platform, his silvery suit gleaming in the afternoon sunlight, and buzzed the crowd. The miners felt the sting of his arrogance and swung at him with their picks and shovels. But they were squat creatures, with short arms.

"You contemptible louts," he said, and performed several acrobatic loops just over their heads to prove they couldn't touch him, but it was a gross miscalculation. A long green arm reached up and snapped shut around his throat.

The Invisible Hand beat his wings frantically, to no avail. He

"Why, it's a blamed mosquito," said one of the miners.

thrashed violently around, but the struggle only tightened the dagger-like grip on his throat.

He was staring into the eyes of a mantid, one of the deadliest bugs in creation. The huge triangular head sported jaws capable of delivering a fatal bite to the largest and deadliest of spiders. What was a mere mosquito to do? Moreover, his silvery suit was being covered in dust, as were his tie pin and cufflinks. That was worse than capture for he had the soul of a dandy. He ceased to struggle.

"You ain't so fancy now," said a miner.

"Nothing but a blamed mosquito," was repeated through the crowd. Mining beetles are not noted for their originality of expression but their feelings are strong. The blamed mosquito had attacked the Angel of the Mines in her big moment with the president of Bugland Rail. "Let's find some flypaper and stick him to it."

"I cannot permit that," said Inspector Mantis. "He will be turned over to the proper authorities."

"There ain't no proper authorities in this town. We'll stick him on flypaper and hang him in the square."

J. Emerson Earwig pushed through the crowd. "Bugland Rail will carry the miscreant to a place of incarceration."

"What's an incarceration?" asked a miner.

"It's where they burn trash," answered another.

"Okay, that'll do."

He was of course thinking of incineration, a satisfactory end for a blamed mosquito who'd insulted the Angel.

Armed guards in the uniform of Bugland Rail came in alongside their boss. Mantis handed over the dapper mosquito. Some miners were still calling for him to be flypapered. So Hopper struck up a tune on his fiddle and nodded to Adora. She began to sing Serenade of the Silkworm, and the miners forgot about flypapering the mosquito.

They made her sing all afternoon. She sang Night of a Thousand Bugs, Lament of the Locust, When I Was in the Cocoon I Dreamed of You, and many more.

"My dear," said J. Emerson Earwig, "you are going to ride back to the capital with me. There I will introduce you to Max Mayfly, owner of the Bugland Follies. Your voice is going to enchant the nation. I will see to that personally."

He escorted her to his private compartment on the train. The Invisible Hand was chained to the floor of the baggage car, which badly wrinkled his suit.

Mantis, Hopper, and Boring Beetle were given their own comfortable compartment. Mantis stared morosely out the window. Hopper saw that now that the case was closed the brooding of Mantis would begin. Without a case to work on he was subject to dark moods. Hopper tried to engage him. "Why were Adora and those other poor ants susceptible to the sound of his wings?"

"Ants are 140 million years old, Hopper. Who knows what encounters they've had, with whom they've interacted, and for what purpose? The sound called forth something deeply buried in the neural ganglia." Mantis took out his pipe and lit it. "Our highflying friend with the humming wings stumbled upon this susceptibility by accident, no doubt. Flying low over the aphid herds perhaps, from whom he wished to suck a bit of nectar. And then, an ant, paralyzed in front of him, her mouth a convenient cup. He puts in his straw and his needs are answered." Smoke curled around the head of Mantis. "I'm sure he took added pleasure from her helplessness, which flattered his vanity. We saw his taste in clothing."

"He's saying he did nothing wrong," replied Hopper.

"The ants he starved to death would say otherwise."

❦ ❂ ❧

THE DUCHESS OF DOODLEBUG applauded the star of the show politely as did other members of Bugland high society. The Duchess cast a critical look at the rowdy miners attending Max Mayfly's New Follies, for they were on their feet cheering Adora Ant. They threw flowers, whistled, slapped each other on the back, slapped perfect strangers on the back, and roared for an encore.

"Really," said the Duchess to the Duke of Doodlebug, "this is too much."

"They love her, my dear," said the Duke. "And I'm quite impressed myself. I don't think I've ever heard such a sweet voice."

"Don't you stand up, Duke. It's inappropriate for one of your rank."

"I'm fastened to my seat," said the Duke, with a wink, which the Duchess did not appreciate. Then she saw Doctor Hopper standing with the miners, along with that very strange fellow, Inspector Mantis. She thought a great deal of the doctor, who had always given her sound medical advice, one piece of which was that she should lighten up a bit, that one can't always be an example of perfect breeding, it wore you out. So she stood.

"My dear," said the Duke, "what's this?"

"Get up, Duke," she said, just as severely as she had told him to remain seated.

Confused but happy to act up a bit, the Duke stood, whistled, and joined the miners in calling for an encore by Adora Ant.

Still the same sweet creature she'd always been, and baffled by the reception she was receiving, she waited until the applause died down and then sang Ballad of the Beggar Tick and Screw Worm Song, the last a heart wrenching offering in a minor key.

Max Mayfly himself came on stage, presenting a huge bouquet to Adora. The Duchess of Doodlebug said to the Duke, "Well, she is a sweet child and did suffer dreadfully from that creature, the Invisible Hat."

"Hand, my dear, the Invisible Hand."

"I'm sure it's Hat."

"Really," said the Duchess to the Duke of Doodlebug, "this is too much."

"Just as you say," said the Duke, who knew better than to argue with his wife.

They met Doctor Hopper in the aisle and she said to him, "Feel my pulse, Doctor. It's bounding beautifully."

"So it is," said Hopper, making a quick check, then asked her to join him, Mantis, and Boring Beetle backstage.

When they got there, Skipjack the new mining millionaire was already talking with Adora. "If not for you, missy, I wouldna heard the mine talkin' to me. And if not for him—" He turned to greet Mantis, "—I wouldna set off the explosion that made my fortune."

The Duchess of Doodlebug stopped in the doorway, looking somewhat critically at the miner who, though now wealthy, still wore the rough dusty clothes of his profession.

"Come on in, honey," he called, "don't be shy."

"Honey?" No one dared call her honey, not even the Duke in their closest moments. She drew herself up stiffly, but Hopper was at her elbow saying softly, "Duchess, your health."

So she entered the dressing room and Skipjack immediately handed her a cup of sparkling nectar. "That'll curl your feelers."

"My feelers are not in need of curling, thank you." But the Duchess sipped the drink, found it to her liking, and had more.

Max Mayfly pushed through the crowd around the dressing room and said, "My friends, tonight a star was born."

Adora Ant sat shyly in front of her dressing room mirror. The Mayfly makeup artist had added so much glamour and glitter to her that she hardly recognized herself.

"We're sold out for the next six months," said Max Mayfly to her, "and all because of this gentleman." He turned to Mantis. "Thank you, sir, for saving her from the Invisible Hand."

"Hat," said the Duchess of Doodlebug, but no one heard her so she had a little more sparkling nectar. It was really quite good.

"Bugland is fortunate to have one such as you," continued Max Mayfly, shaking the hand of the great investigator.

"My friends, tonight a star was born."

"And," said Skipjack, "he knows how to blow a vein of gold."

The dressing room grew more crowded when a group of young dance flies arrived, saying how much they adored Adora Ant. The nectar flowed freely. Songs were sung and the Duke of Doodlebug was astonished to hear his wife harmonizing with Skipjack on Drill Beetles Drill.

Doctor Hopper was not one to leave a party, but in the midst of festivities, Inspector Mantis slipped away with Boring Beetle.

"Well, old man, what's next?" asked Boring Beetle, as they stepped out onto the avenue.

"Crime is everywhere, Boring Beetle. It will come to us."

"And we will meet it gladly. A bug must have adventure or he loses the spice of life. I believe I mentioned nearly being boiled alive in Pandorus?"

"You did." Mantis steeled himself.

"It was a close one. The pot was actually boiling. I was in a hut bound by thick cords. The women of the village came and seasoned me. They told me I'd be delicious. I'd been in tight spots before but never had I been on the menu…"

And the two friends walked on through pools of lamplight, as bugs on either side of them fell into the gutter.

{ ☼ }

Like the first collection of the Inspector Mantis Mysteries,
designed by Kathleen Westray and published in 1975,
Double Trouble in Bugland is set in Linotype Caledonia,
a classic face based on the designs of the transitional faces
of William Martin and adapted by the great American
calligrapher and graphic designer William Addison Dwiggins.
However, in the forty years since the original volume was
issued, technology has radically transformed typesetting.
Rather than cast in slugs of hot metal, the book has been
made-up in Adobe InDesign CS5, with the text set
in Linotype's New Caledonia LT, and Caravan LH
by Michael Babcock at interrobang letterpress,
Jamaica Plain, Massachusetts,
in June 2016.

❄{☼}❄

The book was printed and bound by Toppan in China.